"You're pregnant," Niccolò observed raggedly. "Yet I have only just found out. Why didn't you contact me?"

"Are you kidding?" Lizzie questioned. "I tried! So many times. Soon after the second pregnancy test came back positive and I knew it was really happening, I set out to get in touch with you, but I encountered a setback every step of the way."

"What are you talking about?" he snapped.

"Think about it. You're a very powerful man, Niccolò, and you have a very protective ring of staff surrounding you. That's why I ended up writing you that letter and sending it by snail mail."

"Which I have only just received!" he exploded, pulling a crumpled sheet of paper from the pocket of his overcoat and waving it in front of her.

"Maybe you need to speak to your team of assistants about relaxing their draconian methods of protecting you," she suggested, before biting her lip. "If you recall, we didn't even exchange phone numbers."

Sharon Kendrick once won a national writing competition by describing her ideal date: being flown to an exotic island by a gorgeous and powerful man. Little did she realize that she'd just wandered into her dream job! Today, she writes for Harlequin, and her books feature often stubborn but always to-die-for heroes and the women who bring them to their knees. She believes that the best books are those you never want to end. Just like life...

Books by Sharon Kendrick

Harlequin Presents

Cinderella's Christmas Secret
One Night Before the Royal Wedding
Secrets of Cinderella's Awakening
Confessions of His Christmas Housekeeper
Her Christmas Baby Confession
Innocent Maid for the Greek
Italian Nights to Claim the Virgin

Jet-Set Billionaires

Penniless and Pregnant in Paradise

Passionately Ever After...

Stolen Nights with the King

Visit the Author Profile page at Harlequin.com for more titles.

Sharon Kendrick

—

THE HOUSEKEEPER'S ONE-NIGHT BABY

Recycling programs
for this product may
not exist in your area.

ISBN-13: 978-1-335-59279-8

The Housekeeper's One-Night Baby

Copyright © 2023 by Sharon Kendrick

For questions and comments about the quality of this book,
please contact us at CustomerService@Harlequin.com.

Harlequin Enterprises ULC
22 Adelaide St. West, 41st Floor
Toronto, Ontario M5H 4E3, Canada
www.Harlequin.com

Printed in U.S.A.

THE HOUSEKEEPER'S
ONE-NIGHT BABY

This book is in memory of my adorable cousin, Jennifer Shepherd. She introduced me to music, had the most demure (yet mischievous) smile and was such an enduring inspiration—not just to me and all her other cousins, but especially to her three amazing children: Denise, Roli and Danni.

PROLOGUE

'LEAVING?' LIZZIE'S FINGERS tightened around the phone and a pebble of fear hit the pit of her stomach as she listened to her employer's words. 'I… I don't understand.'

'It's quite simple, Lizzie.' Sylvie's cut-crystal accent slowed as if she were talking to someone very stupid. 'The house is going to have to be sold. There's someone coming to look at it next week, as it happens. That's the beginning and the end of it, I'm afraid.'

'But…' Lizzie's words tailed off as the fear inside her grew heavier.

There were things she wanted to say but she didn't know how, because she wasn't the sort of person who was confident about logical argument—especially with employers. She knew her boundaries. She was good at dusting and cleaning, and painting pictures of animals—dogs, preferably. She'd been brought up never to question the person who was paying your cheque, because security was all-important.

But Sylvie *hadn't* paid her, had she? Lizzie had been subsisting on what remained of her savings for months. Meanwhile her boss had been vague in that charming way the upper classes had—of making you feel as if you should be grateful for what seemed like their friendship. Only it wasn't *really* friendship. A friend would never leave you high and dry with barely any warning. A friend would never take advantage of you without a second thought. She sucked in a deep breath.

So tell her. Make her realise what this means to you.

'But that means I won't have anywhere to live,' she objected quietly.

Sylvie injected a note of faux understanding into her plummy voice. 'I realise that,' she said consolingly. 'But you're a hard worker, Lizzie. You're bound to find a job with accommodation, just like you did with me. And I'll write you a glowing reference, you can be sure of that. There's really nothing to worry about.'

Lizzie swallowed. This next bit was harder, because her mother had always taught her that talking about money was vulgar. But what price vulgarity if the cupboards were bare? 'But you owe me money,' she croaked, her cheeks flushing hotly. 'I haven't had anything for over three months now.'

'Yes. Bit of a cashflow problem, I'm afraid.

Look, I'm not going to promise something I can't deliver, Lizzie—so how about you have a good hunt around the house and take anything you want, in lieu of payment? None of the antiques, obviously—but you'll find plenty of last season's clothes, which I won't be wearing again. You could flog them on the Internet and make yourself a small fortune—isn't that what people do these days? Listen, darling, I have to go—there's a car waiting. I just want to say thanks for everything, and could you make sure the house is super-tidy for next Wednesday? Someone called Niccolò Macario is coming to buy it, hopefully. Some super-hot Italian billionaire, apparently.' Sylvie gave a throaty laugh. 'What a pity I won't be there.'

CHAPTER ONE

HE HAD HIRED a sleek silver sports car for his stay in England, but, having driven it to the centre of the tiny Cotswolds village, Niccolò decided to park next to the duck pond and then walk the last couple of miles. He was feeling wired. More wired than usual. His nerves were jangled. His heart was racing and his lips were dry. He tried not to give it too much thought. Thinking never helped anything and he should be used to this reaction by now. It always happened on this day. Every year, without fail. A pulse thudded at his temple. Without. Fail.

His footsteps slowed to a halt in front of the imposing house and he looked around, trying to appreciate the beauty of his surroundings as the sun beat down on his head. The ancient building which rose into the cloudless sky was the colour of honey and cream. The grounds were lush and beautiful. Heavy roses scented the air with their rich perfume and bees buzzed happily in among the colourful flowerbeds. It was the most idyllic of scenes. Rural England at her finest.

He glanced around and his eyes narrowed, because the beauty was an illusion, like so much else in life. It had an unkempt air about it—like a woman who woke up with last night's mascara clinging to her eyes. If you looked closely you could see the peeling paint and scarred window panes. The inevitable creep of weeds not quite disguised by the vibrant hues of the abundant flowers.

His gaze flicked across to the glitter of an ornamental pool and a ragged sigh erupted from somewhere deep in his lungs. The ache in his heart was always at its most intense in the summer— the bright sunlight mocking the darkness which invaded his soul—the loss and guilt as potent as ever, even after all these years. He felt dead inside. As if someone had taken a blowtorch and blasted everything away, leaving him with nothing but a vast emptiness and a sense of futility.

That was why he chose an annual hands-on project like this to supplement an already busy life—a diversion to capture his attention, as well as adding to his considerable fortune. Buying a potentially valuable property took him back to when he'd first started, when he had been hungry to succeed. He didn't need the money any more, but work was a useful focus for his restless spirit. His lips tightened. It could blot out most things if you let it.

He glanced down at his watch and walked towards the door. The agent from the real estate office was supposed to be meeting him here, though there was no sign of his car. Maybe he had walked, too. As he pressed the doorbell, Niccolò thought about what he'd been told about the property. The owner was a wealthy socialite, apparently, and desperate to sell. He gave a calculating smile. Indiscreet of the agent to let that slip, but always good to know from a negotiating standpoint.

He heard the sound of echoing footsteps from inside the house and then the heavy oak door was pulled open and a woman stood there, framed by the darkness of the interior. A strange wraith of a woman with hair the colour of a faded Halloween pumpkin and translucent skin which was dusted with freckles. She wore a gown of rich green silk, which clung to the luscious outline of her body, and her bare arms were strong. The dress, its hem brushing the stone floor, was completely inappropriate for daytime wear—yet somehow it seemed fitting that such a glorious creature would inhabit a residence as old and historic as this.

Her full lips parted as if in shock and Niccolò felt the unexpected punch of desire as he gazed at her. It was powerful and it was potent. The heavy beat of his heart. The tantalising ache of his groin. He wanted to reach out and touch her, to see if her skin could possibly be as soft as it looked and then to trace the outline of her lips with the pad of his thumb and make them tremble. His mouth was dry as he shook his head, in an attempt to bat away his wayward thoughts. Since when had he started hitting on a total stranger? Didn't women always hit on *him*?

He cleared his throat but that did little to quell the tightening sensation in his chest. 'Niccolò Macario,' he explained succinctly, elevating his eyebrows in question, when still she said nothing. 'I believe you're expecting me?'

Lizzie gazed back at the powerful, black-haired figure who was standing in front of her and all the things she'd been trained to say, like: *Good morning, sir. May I help you?* or, *I believe you've come to view the house, sir?* were stubbornly refusing to leave her lips. Her head was spinning and she couldn't move. Literally couldn't speak. She felt disorientated and bewildered. Because… because…

Could this man possibly be *real*?

She blinked at him in disbelief.

It wasn't just that he was exceptionally tall or exceptionally muscular, with ruffled hair as dark as the wing of a crow. Or that her unwilling attention was drawn by his immaculately cut trousers to the powerful thrust of his legs, just as the rippling silk shirt directed her gaze to his honed torso. It wasn't even the glittering jet gaze, or sexy accent—both of which were making goosebumps shiver over her arms. No, it was the way he was looking at her, those hard eyes narrowed and curious. As if he'd just seen something he hadn't been expecting. Something worth looking at. Normally Lizzie would have glanced behind her to check if his attention had been caught by someone else, which of course it would have been.

Except that she knew herself to be alone.

Alone in a grand house which had been her home, but not for much longer, wearing an outrageously expensive dress belonging to her boss, which was gliding over her flesh like a second skin.

As instructed, she'd spent the morning going through Sylvie's wardrobe—trying to work out the potential value of the various outfits and balancing it against the unpaid wages she was owed. Most of the garments had been badly treated— the odd cigarette burn and red-wine stain making them unwearable—but this one had stood out like a beacon. It was a fantasy dress, the sort of thing she wouldn't usually have dreamed of wearing, even if she'd been able to afford it. She always dressed practically and comfortably, both of which suited her humble position in life and her tendency to shrink into the shadows. But something had compelled Lizzie to throw caution to the wind and slither into it, after first removing her bra so that the silky fabric wouldn't reveal any lumps or bumps.

She swallowed. It was the most exquisite thing

she had ever worn. It made her feel different and was obviously making her *look* different, too. Why else was a man like Niccolò Macario seemingly transfixed by her, when usually she barely merited a second glance from members of the opposite sex?

'You *are* expecting me?' he repeated, slight impatience tinging his tone as he glanced over her shoulder. 'Is the estate agent here?'

'No. Not yet.' Her people-pleasing tendency asserted itself and she shot him a sympathetic look. 'He should have been.'

'Yes, he should,' he agreed coldly.

'Maybe he's been delayed.'

'Maybe,' he conceded, the careless flick of his hand indicating that already he was bored with discussions about the agent, before he frowned again. 'But you *are* still selling your house?'

'Oh, yes. Yes, of course,' she replied hastily and was about to enlighten him that it wasn't actually *her* house and she was just the housekeeper, when something stopped her. He had obviously made the incorrect assumption about her status because she was dressed in this glorious emerald concoction, made by one of the world's leading designers. He certainly wouldn't have asked the same question if she'd been clad in the unflattering grey uniform Sylvie had always insisted she wear—'I think it's better when the staff dress like staff, Lizzie. Everyone likes to know where they stand'—or the sturdy black brogues her boss favoured.

'I'm not actually the owner,' she said reluctantly.

'Oh?'

She met the ebony gleam of his eyes and didn't know what made her say it. Was it because she was enjoying being looked at like a woman for once, rather than some drudge of a servant? Being treated as a human being with thoughts and feelings of her own—rather than as a piece of old furniture you could put your feet on.

'I'm…erm…house-sitting,' she blurted out. Which to some extent was true. She certainly wasn't being *paid* to be here, was she? She was poor and would soon be homeless, but right now she wasn't coming across that way, not judging by the way this man was still regarding her—with unmistakable admiration glittering from his beautiful ebony eyes. And suddenly Lizzie found herself wanting to play the game a little longer. To be a woman in an expensive dress without any scary fears about the future. Why shouldn't she act as if she were this man's equal, even if she knew very well she wasn't? 'But I know the property extremely well. I could show you round, if you wanted.' She hesitated. 'Or you go along to the drawing room and wait for the agent in there.'

'I could. But I haven't much time, I need to be back in London this evening.' His voice became matter-of-fact again and Lizzie wondered if she had imagined the ruthless expression which briefly hardened his strong features.

'Right,' she said uncertainly.

'And so I'm happy for you to show me around instead,' he continued, before fixing her with a quizzical smile. 'Unless you have something else you'd rather be doing?'

The impact of that smile was devastating and Lizzie's heart performed a rapid somersault. But that couldn't have been a serious question. Surely he must be aware that most women would have moved heaven and earth to spend time with him. She certainly would. Hell, yes. It wasn't every day that a man like this tumbled into your orbit.

And even though a small voice was warning against being dazzled by all his charisma, she shut her mind to it. She was perfectly qualified to give him a guided tour and hadn't lied about knowing the historic house. Sometimes she thought she knew the place better than Sylvie and, in truth, was miserable at the thought of having to leave. Over the years, Lizzie had made a point of learning about every precious room and artefact as she carefully polished and preserved them, and wasn't this an opportunity to put her knowledge to some good use? To step out of her self-made shadow and shine for once, before she stepped away from the historic splendour for ever?

'No, I haven't got anything else I'd rather be doing,' she said candidly. 'In fact, I happen to have the whole day to myself.'

'Lucky me,' he said softly.

'Erm.' She cleared her throat. 'Please. Come in.'
'Grazie.'

She watched as he inclined his jet-dark head and entered the property and as he passed she could detect the warm scent of bergamot and spice and something else. Something which seemed at odds with his sophisticated appearance. Was she detecting pheromones and a raw and fundamental sex appeal? Suddenly Lizzie wondered if she had bitten off more than she could chew and just as suddenly realised that she *didn't care*.

'L-let's start here, shall we?' she said, hastily beginning to recount the facts about the house which she'd learnt so assiduously. But that wasn't really surprising since she had grown to love Ermecott Manor, almost as if it were her own. 'This is the Great Hall, which was built in the mid-seventeenth century, although the stained-glass windows didn't appear until nearly seventy years later.' She gestured upwards towards the windows—some of which were unfortunately cracked. But the sudden movement caused her unfettered breasts to wobble beneath the delicate silk, reminding her that she was *still wearing Sylvie's dress* and she must look like a complete idiot. Was that why Niccolò Macario gave a short intake of breath, as if someone had suddenly robbed the room of oxygen?

'I'd better go and change into something more suitable,' she said quickly.

Dark eyes met hers. 'Why would you do that?'

'Isn't it obvious?' She gave a nervous laugh. 'It's an evening dress.'

'It is also a very beautiful dress, which makes you blend into these ancient surroundings perfectly,' he commented sagely. 'Certainly better than a pair of jeans, which I'm guessing would be your chosen alternative.'

To her horror, Lizzie started blushing at what *sounded* like a compliment, though she didn't exactly have a lot of experience of those either. She hadn't been out with anyone since Dan, who used to delight in putting her down, for reasons best known to himself. Why she had tolerated it for so long was another matter and more to do with her own lack of self-esteem than any magnificent trait possessed by her ex-boyfriend.

Resisting the desire to fan her face and draw attention to her hot cheeks, Lizzie glanced down at the emerald silk which was pooling luxuriously by her feet. No point in enlightening him that she hardly ever wore jeans because she considered her bottom too big, but neither did she want to go upstairs and risk breaking the spell he seemed to have cast over her. She wanted to hang onto this delicious feeling and revel in every second of it, like someone getting into a deep bubble bath at the end of a long day. Lifting her head, she met his ebony gaze and prayed the estate agent wouldn't suddenly ring on the front door.

'You really think it's okay?' she questioned naively.

'I really do,' he replied gravely.

Their gazes met and she couldn't seem to look away and neither, it seemed, could he. She'd never stared at anyone like that before—nor had the feeling that to do so was perfectly okay. It was as if he were exerting some silent and unknown power over her—making her long for things which had always eluded her before.

Her frigidity had been one of Dan's main complaints. *'You're like a block of ice, Lizzie.'* Well, she certainly wasn't feeling like a block of ice now. Her blood was burning through her veins and she could feel her breasts swelling to what felt like twice their normal size, their tips becoming painful little bullets which were pushing against the slippery silk of her gown. Did he notice that? Was that why his body had grown unmistakably tense?

She could feel the silken rush of heat low in her core and she turned away, terrified he would somehow guess the crazy thoughts which were crowding her mind. 'In that case, why don't we get on with the tour?' Her voice was artificially bright as she pointed an unsteady finger down towards one of the corridors leading off the Great Hall. 'We can do the ground floor first.'

'*Perfetto,*' he said, his brief smile almost making her want to weep because he looked so beautiful.

Niccolò followed the bright-haired woman through the shadowed rooms, forcing himself to concentrate on the panelled walls and worn flagstones and the jewel-coloured light spilling through the stained-glass windows. He looked around with a connoisseur's eye and thought how beautiful the bare bones of the house were, and how much better it would look if some money were lavished on it.

'This is the room where the original family chose to eat,' his red-headed guide informed him chattily. 'It gave them a little privacy, away from the watchful eyes of their servants.'

'*Sì*, the ever-watchful eyes of servants,' he observed. 'Though in a house this size it would be impossible not to have them around.'

'Yes, staff can be a bit of a double-edged sword, can't they?' she said, a slightly acid note entering her voice. 'A bit like a trip to the dentist. You know you have to endure them, you just wish you didn't have to.'

Her sharp interjection gave him the excuse he needed to study her again, but he didn't stop to wonder what had motivated it because he was so captivated by the eyes which were gazing up at him. They really were the most extraordinary colour—as green as fresh pistachios and fringed by lashes the same colour as her hair. Her bare lips were curiously inviting and he found himself staring at them for a second longer than was necessary. Was that the reason why—to his unexpected delight—she actually *blushed*?

As if she had revealed too much of herself she turned her back on him, and now he was presented with the equally delectable sway of her buttocks, green silk gleaming enticingly as it moved over the fleshy globes. The pale red hair reached almost to her waist and he wondered how it might feel to run his fingers through the heavy strands. His heart was pounding and suddenly Niccolò felt alive. The bleakness which was clogging his heart seemed to have been granted a temporary amnesty by the sudden urgent needs of his body and he wanted to taste her. To cover those soft lips with his own. Yet the sting of desire was coupled with confusion— because he couldn't recall such a fierce and indiscriminate hunger beyond his teenage years, when his behaviour had been governed by the unstoppable flood of hormones. His mouth hardened. And look what had happened as a result of that.

'Are you looking at this as a family home?' she questioned.

Her words burst the bubble of painful thoughts and he narrowed his eyes in question.

'If…if you decide to buy, I mean,' she added briskly. 'There are…there are lots of good local schools nearby.'

Niccolò knew exactly what she was doing. Trying to establish whether or not he was single. It happened. In fact, it happened a lot of the time. A clumsy query prompted by a fruitless search for the outline of a wedding ring, or the image of a smiling baby on the home screen of his phone. The thought of that made his heart twist and he wanted to recoil with all the hurt which was still inside him, but years of self-discipline enabled him to stem his reaction with a brief tightening of his hands.

'No, I don't have any family,' he clipped out. 'And that situation isn't going to change.'

'Right,' she said.

He knew he'd given her more information than was needed and wondered what had prompted his uncharacteristic disclosure. Was it to make her understand what kind of man he really was? To warn her that, while he acknowledged the powerful and unusual chemistry which was simmering between them, he wasn't looking for a wife to grace this elegant abode. Or anywhere else. 'If you must know, I'm looking for a property to develop in southern England.'

'*Develop?*' The word triggered an instant reaction and she was staring at him as if he had just proposed conducting a sacrificial rite beneath the beamed ceilings of the ancient building. 'You can't do that!' she blustered indignantly.

'Why not?'

'Because this is a Grade I listed property and

there are strict rules concerning what you can and can't do with it.'

'What do you imagine I want to do with it?' he demanded sarcastically. 'Build a three-storey extension on the side and put in an underground swimming pool?'

'I don't know—you tell me!' she flared back, as if he had touched a raw nerve. 'We have far too many people coming to this part of the world, flashing their cash and trying to...'

'Trying to what?' he questioned as her words tailed away.

She shook her head, as if she had said too much. 'It doesn't matter.'

'No, tell me. I'm curious.' And he was, despite the fact that people rarely spoke to him with such insulting candour.

She shrugged and, in the subdued lighting, the dark green straps of her dress shimmered. 'To change things.'

'And you don't like change?'

'Does anyone?' She seemed to remember that she was supposed to be helping sell her friend's house and shrugged. 'Well, I don't mind the changes we're in control of.'

Was there any such thing? Niccolò wondered. He thought of his dead sister. Of his mother. And the father who had never bothered to hide his contempt for him after the accident. He thought of a simple decision which could have changed the whole course of everybody's lives, his own included—and how the nightmare would never have happened. But nobody could rewrite the past—no matter how much they wanted to, he reminded himself bitterly. It was the present which should be concerning him.

'I'm not planning a major assault on a much-loved landmark building. I'm not totally without taste or sensitivity,' he said quietly, because he wanted to wipe that melancholic expression from her face.

'What are you planning to do with it, then?' she ventured curiously, before adding, 'If you buy it, that is.'

He curved her a smile. 'Why don't you have dinner with me tonight and I'll tell you?'

Lizzie blinked at him, not sure if she'd heard him correctly. Was he actually asking her *out*? On a *date*? 'You want to have dinner with me?'

'Is that such a wild proposition?'

Well, of course it was. Things like that didn't happen to women like her. She wondered what might have happened next if the shrill ring of the doorbell hadn't echoed through the house and they both froze, as if stunned by the sound of the outside world.

'It's the agent,' she whispered, peering out through the window to see a familiar figure.

'Don't answer it,' he whispered back.

'He's…he's got a key. He'll let himself in.'

'So let's hide,' he suggested silkily. 'And maybe he'll go away.'

There was a heartbeat of a pause while Lizzie weighed up the wisdom of such an action. No way should they be hiding away, like a couple of kids. Niccolò Macario shouldn't be suggesting it and she certainly shouldn't be colluding with it. But she knew what would happen the moment the agent walked in. He would see her—not clad in her habitual frumpy grey dress and sensible shoes, but shimmying around in one of Sylvie's more expensive cast-offs.

And it wasn't just his expression she was dreading—one of disbelief, quickly followed by suspicion, and a faint concern that she'd lost her marbles, or was in the process of stealing something. No, it would be the way he would behave which she couldn't face. With that slightly patronising air which was so hard to take sometimes. Because it didn't matter how liberal or nice people considered themselves to be, they always treated domestic staff differently. Sometimes they were a little *too* friendly, sometimes they were aloof, but one thing was for sure, they were never *normal*. They probably didn't even realise they were doing it, but it always made her feel small. Like a second-class citizen.

And she didn't want to feel that way in front of Niccolò Macario. She wanted to carry on pretending they were equals, with him looking at her with undisguised pleasure in his black eyes. With her revelling in the thought that he had actually asked her to have dinner with him and she still hadn't told him yes, or no.

'Okay,' she said breathlessly. 'Follow me.' Scarcely able to believe what she was doing, she walked towards a small broom cupboard at the far end of the corridor and stepped inside, clicking on the low-wattage bulb, which brought only a meagre element of light to the cramped space. Her throat dried as Niccolò followed her and the quiet click of the door closed them off from the world, muffling the sound of the agent's voice as he called out her name.

'Lizzie!' And then again, louder this time. *'Lizzie!'*

But Lizzie didn't answer. She just stood there, not moving, barely breathing—though her heart was beating so loudly she was certain Niccolò must be able to hear it.

'This is ridiculous,' she whispered, at one point.

'So what if it is?' He gave a short laugh. 'Isn't the very substance of life ridiculous?'

She couldn't think of an answer to that cynical query, because that was the moment the agent chose to pass right by the cupboard and Lizzie held her breath, her skin turning to goosebumps as she met the dark glitter of Niccolò's mocking stare.

It was very small in here, she thought. Much too confined for two people to be able to stand there and avoid touching. But that was what it felt like they were doing, even though they weren't actually *touching*. It was as if they were in a bubble, all of their own. He was close enough for her to be able to detect his body heat, and be acutely aware of his breathing. Close enough for him to see her erect nipples, outlined boldly against the emerald silk, and she couldn't seem to shift the inappropriate thought that she wanted him to stroke them. She wanted that very badly and that kind of raw hunger and urgent need had never happened to her before.

She didn't know how long they stood there, while the hapless agent continued to call her name. Only that the tension seemed to increase with every second which passed—especially when she heard the faint vibrating sound of Niccolò's phone, coming from his pocket. She saw his eyes widen but he didn't move and she prayed the agent wouldn't have super-sensitive hearing and come charging back down the corridor. She imagined him opening the door and finding them and, if that were the case, what on earth would they *say*?

But there was nothing except the sound of retreating footsteps and after a while the front door slammed and the sound of an accelerating car informed her that they were alone once more.

Their gazes met. The tension broke and they burst out laughing, at exactly the same time. It was a heady rush of pure adrenaline. A unique moment of shared communication, acknowledging their complicity. But when the laughter died away, the tension was back, only this time it was different. It was so powerful it was almost tangible. It was all-consuming—but most of all, it was physical. Her senses were on fire. She ached with a desire and heat which was drenching her core. She felt dizzy with the sensation—helpless yet energised, all at the same time.

'Now what?' he questioned softly.

Lizzie wasn't experienced enough to know what he meant yet somehow she knew exactly what he meant. She ought to move. Open the door and let some daylight in. Say something bright and superficial which would make everything seem normal again.

But she didn't move.

Didn't speak.

She just waited for something she knew shouldn't be happening, which she wanted. So much. Because the weirdest thing was that somehow she felt *connected* to this man. As if this meeting was in some way predestined and everything was exactly as it should be. Was it the dress which was making her feel so decadent? The sensation of cool silk coating her skin like honey and making her feel like a real woman for once, instead of a common skivvy? Or was it that Niccolò Macario was the most gorgeous man she'd ever met and she felt as if she were in the middle of some amazing dream, with all kinds of possibilities?

Life had been tough for Lizzie. She'd grown up with more responsibilities than most of her peers. She'd learned to put everyone else first and place her own needs last, but for once she wanted to do something for herself. Something incredible. Just for the hell of it. A dinner date was a stretch too far. She'd feel far too self-conscious in a posh restaurant and he would quickly discover she wasn't who he thought she was. And then he would be disappointed.

But right here was perfect for what she wanted right now.

Feeling a bit like Cinderella, she gazed up into the ebony glitter of his eyes.

Kiss me, she prayed silently. *Just kiss me.*

CHAPTER TWO

THE WOMAN HE now knew to be Lizzie was breath-takingly close and Niccolò knew he needed to get out of this damned broom cupboard before it was too late and he did something he regretted. His heart pounded. But she wanted him to kiss her. There was no mistake about that. Her eyes were wide and dark with longing and the sexual hunger radiating from her curvy body was instantly apparent. She looked sweet and desirable.

He shook his head, trying to hammer some logic into his befuddled brain, because he was responsible for the position in which he now found himself. He had made an impetuous suggestion and, to his surprise, the redhead had agreed to it. Yet he didn't *do* impetuous and he'd never had sex with a stranger before—a prospect which was becoming more likely with every passing second. It wasn't even something he'd ever considered—and he certainly wouldn't have chosen this most unlikely of settings, with a feather duster dangling inconveniently nearby and some sort of mop and bucket in the corner.

Yet something nebulous drew him to the curvy little guide. Something which transcended her pale green eyes and translucent skin. He had laughed uninhibitedly with her as they'd hidden from the hapless agent, and that was rare for a man known to be sombre. It had felt like the most potent of aphrodisiacs. Like a fierce light flooding his darkened soul. That it should have happened on this, the worst day of his calendar year, made it even more significant. Did that explain the exquisite hardness in his groin and the pulsing slug of his blood? His heart was beating erratically as he stared down into her face, a fast-dwindling sense of rationality silently imploring her to warn him off. 'I want to kiss you,' he said unevenly.

There was a pause while he waited for an outrage he knew deep down wouldn't materialise. Yet part of him had wanted her to refuse him, because it would be far simpler to beat a hasty retreat. To go back to his hotel room and blot out the rest of the day with a glass, or three of whisky. But no, she tilted her face upwards so that her soft lips were a mere breath away.

'Well, that's handy, because I want you to kiss me,' she whispered.

'Are you sure?' His voice was deliberately hard. 'You should be careful what you wish for, *cara*.'

'Why?'

Did she realise that the near innocence of her question was completely at odds with the blatant sensuality of the foxy dress she was wearing? Or perhaps she was aware that men were turned on by apparent contradictions and was capitalising on that. 'Because once we start kissing you're going to want to have sex with me,' he drawled. 'And you need to decide if that's really such a good idea.'

Her lashes lowered to shade her widened eyes, but her expression was composed when they fluttered open again, as if she had just given herself a silent pep talk. 'You're very sure of yourself, aren't you?'

'With women?' He shrugged. 'Always.'

He wanted her to rail against him for his perceived arrogance—when all he was doing was stating a fact—but she didn't. There wasn't a trace of recrimination on her freckled face. Instead, her lips were parting in as blatant an invitation as he'd ever seen and the glint of hunger in her eyes was unmistakable as she swayed towards him.

And now it was too late for caution or warning, because his own needs had taken over and he was kissing her and she was kissing him back with a fervour which took his breath away. And her lips tasted incredible. *Incredible.* Niccolò gave a small groan. *Madre di Dio.* Like honey and silk.

Her hair felt like silk too, and he ran his fingers through the luxuriant strands as he'd wanted to do from the first moment he'd seen her. Cupping her face, he deepened the kiss until she was moaning with soft abandon, her hands clutching at his shoulders—and that was all the leverage he needed. He brought her even closer so that her breasts were pressing into him, the hardened tips jutting provocatively against his chest and he closed his eyes as spears of desire made his groin grow rocky. He thought about unzipping himself and plunging deep inside her molten heat and he almost gasped aloud with the anticipation of that.

Still, he offered her another chance to call a halt to this madness as he dragged his lips away from hers. 'If you want to change your mind,' he managed unsteadily, 'now might be the moment.'

'No,' she whispered, shaking her head so that her bright hair glimmered in the dim light. 'I don't.'

His throat tightened and relief rushed over him as he caressed a thrusting nipple between his finger and his thumb.

'So. Are you going to take me upstairs?' he questioned silkily as she squirmed with pleasure.

Lizzie struggled to steady her breath as she met the glitter in Niccolò's eyes. Her heart was beating faster than she could ever remember, her body was on fire with need but she was afraid to move—terrified that the journey between this tiny alcove and the bedroom would destroy the magic they had created.

Because what if he changed his mind on the

way? What if she did? That would obviously be the most sensible option, but right now she didn't want to feel sensible. She felt almost...*wild*—and that wasn't like her at all. But she had played safe all her life and where had it got her? Stony broke and soon to be homeless, that was where. What did she have to lose? She had always been a good girl but suddenly she wanted to be bad. Really, really bad. Surely that wasn't such a major crime.

'Upstairs? It's a bit of a trek.' Rising up on tiptoes, she trailed her lips over the darkened rasp of his jaw and her throaty response came out of its own accord, as if she were the type of woman who whispered flirtatious questions to strange men every day of the week. 'Is that what you want?'

His breath was shuddering as he took her hand and placed it over his heart, its fierce thunder easily matching her own. She could see tension tautening his strong features as he bit the words out, his Italian accent suddenly very pronounced. 'What do you *think* I want, Lizzie?'

She hoped he wasn't hoping for a coherent answer because she couldn't give one. Couldn't do anything except gasp out her undisguised pleasure as he brushed his hand slowly over her swollen breast and the nipple peaked against his palm. He made a low murmur of appreciation but his hand did not stop to linger and Lizzie closed her eyes with expectation as he skimmed his fingers over her hips and began to ruck up the silken dress.

'Oh,' she gasped as a questing forefinger found her bare leg and tiptoed up her inner thigh, only he took so long about it that she thought she was going to lose her mind. At last it reached her panties and she heard him mutter something appreciative as he encountered the moist heat, which must have seared against him. She gave a little cry as he edged the damp fabric aside and touched her aroused flesh and she was scarcely aware of the feather duster brushing against her bare shoulders as she leaned back against the wall, while he began to strum her with sweet precision. And then things got heated. The pleasure was building and building, sweet and intense. She couldn't stop it, even if she wanted to. She bit her lip. And sweet heaven—how could she ever want to stop something like this?

'Niccolò,' she crooned restlessly.

'Tell me,' he coaxed, fractionally increasing the pressure.

But she couldn't answer. All she could do was cry out as she started to orgasm, her body bucking helplessly beneath his finger, and he smothered her lips with his own and kissed her. And only when she had quietened and the spasms had faded did he draw away from her. In the dim light, he brushed her hair away from her face and she could detect her musky scent on his fingertips. His gaze was jet-dark and piercing as it sliced into her and his breathing was quickened, but it was hard to tell from his expression what was going on in his head.

'I want to be inside you, Lizzie,' he said silkily. 'I want that very much. But not in here, with a damned broom sticking into my back. Do you want to take me upstairs now?'

His tone was as calm and as logical as if he were putting a proposition to a debating society—making it sound as if she had some sort of choice in the matter when she felt as if she would go mad if he didn't possess her completely. She wondered how he could be so *controlled* when her blood was practically at boiling point. She wondered again what he was thinking but she sensed she would never know.

It made sense to move but where did she take him? Not up to her room, that was for sure. If he thought the broom cupboard was claustrophobic, he'd get a shock when he saw her tiny eaves room at the very top of the house, with its single bed and sloping ceiling. She wouldn't use Sylvie's room for obvious reasons—she didn't want to look at her boss's haughty portrait staring down at her as she lay on the bed with Niccolò. She thought about the Red Room—which was the best of all the guest rooms and a little bit decadent, as its name suggested. And since she was the one responsible for keeping it clean and tidy—what did it matter if they mussed it up a little?

'Okay,' she said huskily. 'Come with me.'

Slowly, she ascended the dark wooden staircase, trying not to focus too deeply on what she was about to do. She pushed open the door into a room resplendent with heavy red velvet and satin. There were swags and fringes and thick golden brocade and as Niccolò followed her inside, she remembered the time one of Sylvie's drunken guests had proclaimed that it looked like a bordello. Did it?

She watched him walk over to the window and look out at the overgrown gardens and suddenly she remembered that he was here as a prospective buyer and her thoughts shot off on an unexpected trajectory. What if he *did* buy it? Would he need a housekeeper? And if so had she just destroyed her chances of getting the job by letting him bring her to orgasm in the broom cupboard?

But that mass of crazy possibilities dissolved when he crossed the room and took her in his arms again, staring down into her face with an unfathomable expression before he dipped his head, so that his warm breath fanned her lips.

'Now,' he murmured. 'Where were we?'

Her head tipped back and suddenly she was shy and out of her depth. Wasn't she supposed to be a frigid virgin? she wondered dazedly. 'I… I can't remember.'

'Then perhaps I'd better remind you.'

He started with a kiss, then slowly trailed his lips all the way down her neck, until his tongue reached her cleavage and Lizzie gave a little moan of pleasure as he traced a moist line between her breasts. With a low and unsteady laugh, he unzipped her dress and it slithered to the ground in a whisper of heavy silk as he took a step back to look at her. But oddly, Lizzie didn't feel in the least bit self-conscious as she stood in front of him, wearing nothing but her panties.

Was that because his dark gaze was sweeping over her body with blatant admiration, or because she felt as if she were on the brink of something extraordinary? As if everything which had happened in her world up until now had happened for a reason. And this was the reason. Him. This man with whom she felt a powerful connection which was more than just physical. She was aware of helping unbutton his shirt with fingers which were unusually shaky, and that he was having some difficulty sliding the zip of his trousers down. Maybe that should have daunted her, but it didn't because, unexpectedly, he told her she was beautiful as he kicked away his handmade leather shoes and, even though she knew she wasn't, he actually made her *believe* it.

And nothing could have prepared her for the joy of being naked in his arms once they were lying on the bed together, as if that were a perfectly normal thing to do. Or revelling in the silken texture of his warm skin against hers. The contrast of the hard planes and sinews of his body against the softness of her own was nothing short of intoxicating.

She grew bolder by the second, her fingers beginning to explore him—edging over his chest and down over his hard belly. But when she tentatively tiptoed towards his groin, he said something fervent in Italian and shook his dark head, reaching for a small packet on the bedside table, which he must have put there, unnoticed by her. But then his face hardened, and he tilted her chin so that their gazes were on a collision course.

'It is not too late,' he ground out.

'T-too late for what?' she echoed unsteadily.

'To call a halt to this madness.' His lips twisted in an odd kind of smile. 'For that is what it is.'

He might as well have held up a written warning, but Lizzie paid his words no heed. How could she? She'd read about the point of no return plenty of times, where foreplay had gone too far to be able to stop. Another wave of longing rippled through her. This must be it.

'No,' she said, through lips so swollen with his kiss that the words sounded slurred. 'I don't want to stop. Unless…' She forced herself to say it. 'Unless you do.'

He growled with what sounded like anticipation. 'What do you think, Lizzie?' He buried his lips in her hair as he moved on top of her, all muscle and skin and warm weight. 'Oh Lizzie,' he whispered. And then he was inside her. With one thrust he filled her with his hardness and she cried out, mostly in wonder that something could be so intimate. She could feel her body expanding to accommodate him—and after that initial pierce of pain it felt nothing short of amazing. She was briefly aware of him growing still inside her, but she was too intent on her own needs to pay it any attention.

'Please,' she whimpered instinctively.

'Please what?' he husked.

'M-more.'

He gave another growl as he began to move again and she angled her hips to meet his powerful thrust—slow and provocative at first until it increased in urgency. The tension inside her began to build as wild excitement gripped her, and this time she knew what to expect. She felt his big body shudder in time with hers and Lizzie was overcome by a feeling of utter contentment as he gave a shout of something which sounded shaken, and exultant.

In that dreamy state, she must have fallen asleep because she was woken by the unwelcome sensation of him withdrawing from her body, though already he was hard again. She opened her eyes to object to find herself confronted by a searing black gaze and apprehension spiked at her skin like needles. It wasn't exactly a *hostile* look, but it wasn't what she was expecting. What *was* she expecting? That he would slowly raise her fingertips to his lips and tell her he'd just found the woman of his dreams?

Before, his expression had been filled with passion and appreciation—but now… Now he was surveying her with an expression she couldn't work out.

'Niccolò?' she questioned uncertainly.

Niccolò raked his long fingers back through the disarray of his thick hair, trying to make some sense of what had just happened. He'd just had sex with a stranger. A virgin. A sweet, tight, passionate virgin. 'That was *not* what I was expecting,' he husked, his heart still racing as he stared at her, in all her ruffled beauty, as she lay outlined against a pillow of scarlet and golden brocade. 'Why the hell didn't you say something?'

'You mean…' the tiny tip of a very pink tongue touched the edges of her lips '…that you were the first?'

He gave a short laugh. 'What else would I mean?'

'You didn't…' Her voice faltered. 'You didn't like it?'

His eyes narrowed. He didn't *think* she was being disingenuous, but with women you could never be sure. 'You know damned well I did,' he bit out, before expelling a heavy sigh. 'But you shouldn't have wasted your innocence on a man like me.'

She was regarding him with bewilderment. 'Wasted it?'

Did she really need him to spell it out for her? 'If you've waited this long, then you should have chosen a man with whom you want to have a relationship—and that man isn't going to be me, *cara*.'

There was a pause, but she didn't take the hint. 'You're saying you don't have relationships?'

He shook his head. Not with women who had eyes he could drown in. Who kissed him as if they'd never been kissed before. Who could make him forget his pain and his grief but leave something in its place which made him uneasy. 'Not with people who live on the other side of the world.' He gave her an apologetic smile. 'Nothing personal. I just don't have the time.'

'Okay. Well, thanks for being straight with me. I…appreciate it.' She sat up straight and began to slide her legs towards the edge of the bed and, although he could see it was an effort, she slanted him the sweetest smile. 'I guess there's nothing more to be said.'

Was it her generosity which made his mind race—a generosity he probably didn't deserve? Or just the realisation that she was taking him at his word and preparing to leave and, as she stood up, all he could see was the rosy tightness of her nipples and the pale triangle of fire at the juncture of her thighs? And suddenly his thinking brain was no longer functioning efficiently as the rush of blood was diverted towards the more elemental requirements of his body.

'Or we could spend the rest of the night together,' he said slowly.

She turned her head, her green gaze clashing with his. 'Haven't you got to be back in London tonight?' Clearly not making it easy for him.

'Yes, I was going to a business dinner, but I can make my excuses. I want to make love to you again,' he told her softly. 'There are so many things I would like to do to you, which I think you would enjoy. But I meant what I said.' He paused and said the words very deliberately, just so there could be no misunderstanding. 'No strings. No expectations. What do you say to that, Lizzie?'

Her lashes had lowered and her cheeks had grown very pink and at that moment she looked every inch the virgin she had been until very recently. He wondered if she would respond with outrage. He wondered, achingly, whether she would prove to be the exception of every other woman he'd ever known and refuse him. But when she looked up he could see the answer written in the sensual softening of her features.

'I say yes,' she whispered shyly. 'I'd like that very much.'

CHAPTER THREE

Six months later

LIZZIE WAS BENDING over the ironing board, pressing what felt like her hundredth shirt of the day when she heard the sound of the doorbell and she sighed. Sometimes the steep steps leading up from the basement of the grand house to the front door made her feel as if she were scaling Mount Everest. She got so very tired these days, yet sleep was increasingly hard to come by—such were the downsides of her condition. But she mustn't concentrate on the negatives, she reminded herself firmly. She needed to remember her gratitude list. Her pregnancy was progressing extremely well and she was lucky to have a job, in the circumstances.

But her mental list had petered out as she reached the entrance hall, her footfall noiseless on the silken Persian rug. She wondered who was calling at this time in the morning. Her boss was out but even if she'd been at home, Lizzie doubted whether any of her friends would have just dropped by to say hello. Spontaneity wasn't a word she associated with the upper classes.

It was cold up here, because the heating was kept off during the day while she was working and Lizzie shivered as she opened the front door. But the blast of cold air in wasn't responsible for the sudden icing of her skin, or the frozen horror of her reaction as her shocked gaze alighted on Niccolò Macario standing on the doorstep, blocking out most of the light behind him, his features set and forbidding.

Last time she'd seen him it had been summer, when the sun had transformed him into a glowing golden god—whereas today he was outlined in stark shades of monochrome, against the bare landscape of winter. Her heart raced. Actually, that wasn't strictly true. The last time she'd seen him he had only recently been thrusting deep inside her and she had slithered back into Sylvie's—now very rumpled—green dress. And if he'd wondered why she hadn't thrown on a dressing gown, or a pair of jeans to see him off the premises, he hadn't asked and she hadn't been required to tell him that her clothes were all upstairs in the box room, not the fancy scarlet guest room. But then, they hadn't asked each other any questions, had they? They'd been too busy exploring each other's bodies as the clock had ticked the night away into a sleepless morning.

She dragged in an unsteady breath as she stared at him. For a long while she'd wondered how she could have behaved in such an impetuous way, with a man she barely knew. It had been hard not to beat herself up about it but as she looked at him now her error of judgement became a lot more understandable. He was, she thought, her throat drying to dust, still the most magnificent man she'd ever laid eyes on.

She had fallen for him big time but, clearly, he hadn't felt the same way about her and a whole night together hadn't changed his determination that there would be no strings, or expectations. But she wouldn't have been human if she hadn't held out a little hope that he might change his mind. She'd wondered if she might bump into him again and, if she did, whether that overpowering chemistry would lead them straight back to the bedroom. Another no-hoper, because the Jacobean mansion had sold a few weeks later—but not to him. Ermecott Manor had been bought by a family from Scotland who had brought their own housekeeper with them, leaving her looking for a job. That she had found one in the circumstances had been something of a miracle. And the question which was looming large was how had Niccolò found *her*, especially as she was now living in London? And why, when he had gone out of his way to avoid her?

She looked him directly in the eye, trying to

make him focus on her face and not her body—though instinct told her this was a pointless exercise.

'Good morning, Niccolò,' she said calmly, somehow managing to keep the tell-tale waver of emotion from her voice. 'I must say, this is a surprise.'

'I imagine it must be,' he replied. 'You took some tracking down, *cara*.' There was a pause, while his black eyes narrowed. 'And you seem to have no presence at all on the Internet.'

'You're right, I haven't,' she agreed. She wasn't registered on any of the social media channels. She didn't post carefully filtered photographs of herself online, desperate for other people's approval. She didn't have the time, even if she'd ever had the inclination. She drew in a deep breath. 'Anyway, surely that's irrelevant. What are you doing here?'

'Isn't it obvious?' At last his gaze swept over her, from head to toe, his lips hardening as it returned to linger on the curve of her belly, which was pushing against the checked beige tabard, which was her latest housekeeper uniform. 'And surely it's a little late in the day for maidenly blushing.'

She wanted to slam the door in his face, but she knew she couldn't do that and not just because his expression was so flinty. She wasn't an unreasonable person and she hoped that, when the chips were down, neither was he. She couldn't hold

his behaviour against him just because he hadn't
wanted to see her again. And hadn't this brand-
new life growing inside her given her the kind of
self-belief and courage she'd never had before?
Wasn't she a much stronger woman now there was
someone else to consider?

*So find out what he wants and then decide how
you're going to deal with it.*

She would take him downstairs into the basement and after he'd finished saying his piece, he
could slip out of the kitchen door and nobody
would even know he'd been here. She opened the
door wider.

'Come in,' she said. 'Though you'll have to be
quick. My boss will be back soon.'

Niccolò didn't answer. He didn't trust himself
to say another word as he stepped in and shut the
door behind him, still reeling from the sight of her,
which was affecting him in ways he couldn't begin
to understand. In silence he followed her down a
flight of stairs, into the lavish subterranean basement kitchen. But it was cold in here, he thought
critically, and found himself wondering if she was
warm enough.

She turned round and once again he was
shocked by her appearance. Not just because her
dark-ringed eyes suggested chronic tiredness—
though the bright hair piled on top of her head
looked thicker than he remembered—but because
of the very obvious signs of her pregnancy. It was

strange. You could know something to be a fact, but it wasn't until you were actually confronted with the evidence that you really started to believe it was true. And this was true all right. His throat grew dry as he scanned her abdomen, for beneath the ugly garment she wore he could see the unmistakable sign of a bump.

His child.

A child he had never wanted.

Pain speared at his heart. And guilt. That everpresent sense of guilt. And something else, too. Something he didn't recognise. Something he didn't want to recognise. 'You're pregnant,' he observed raggedly.

'Six months,' she offered.

'Yet I have only just found out. Why the hell didn't you contact me?'

'Are you kidding?' she questioned. 'I tried! So many times. Soon after the second pregnancy test came back positive and I knew it was really happening, I set out to get in touch with you, but I encountered a setback every step of the way. I had no alternative other than to try to contact you through your company, which meant I was always onto a loser.'

'What are you talking about?' he clipped out.

'Think about it,' she accused. 'You're a very powerful man, Niccolò and you have a very protective ring of staff surrounding you. You're a billionaire and I'm just a humble working girl. Gaining access to you was a bit like someone trying to get their hands on the Crown Jewels. That's why I ended up writing you that letter and sending it by snail mail.'

'Which I have only just received!' he exploded, pulling a crumpled sheet of paper from the pocket of his overcoat and waving it in front of her. 'And you're no longer living at the address on the letter, hence the difficulty in finding you.'

'Maybe you need to speak to your team of assistants about relaxing their draconian methods of protecting you,' she suggested, before biting her lip. 'If you recall, we didn't even exchange phone numbers, which was another complicating factor, otherwise I could have tried you at home or texted you, or *something*.'

'I thought we'd decided that was for the best.'

'Well, *you* decided that,' she argued.

'Because what happened that day was a crazy aberration between two people living on opposite sides of the world!'

'Yes, of course there were practical reasons why we weren't going to see each other again, but they weren't the only ones, were they?' Her gaze sliced through him, as pale as new leaves. 'Do you remember what you said to me, or shall I remind you? *"No strings. No expectations."* Those were your exact words, weren't they, Niccolò—or has pregnancy scrambled my brain so much that I can no longer rely on my own memory?'

'I was trying to do you a favour,' he said harshly. 'I didn't want you building up any unrealistic romantic dreams about me.'

'I was hardly likely to do that. A broom cupboard is hardly the most romantic of settings.' She gave a short laugh. 'I mean, we're not exactly talking Romeo and Juliet here, are we?'

'You wanted it,' he said softly.

There was a pause as her cheeks flushed and when she spoke, her voice was so low he could barely hear it. 'You're saying you didn't?'

He shook his head before biting out the words reluctantly. 'Of course I did.' He wondered how she would react if he told her that the desire he'd felt for her had been off the scale. That he'd never felt anything like that before in his life. Wild. Hungry. Out of control. Hadn't that realisation been a bigger incentive to make him resist the temptation to see her again than the perceived incompatibility of their two lifestyles? And that had been when he'd thought she was a rich socialite, not a woman actually working in the house. He gave a heavy sigh. 'If you'd told me you were a virgin, you wouldn't have seen me for dust.'

'I didn't get the chance, did I? We didn't exactly do a lot of talking.'

He could hear the tremble of something in her voice. Was it anger or was it hurt? 'No,' he said, at last. 'We didn't.'

'Oh, well. At least we know where we stand

now. It's hardly ground-breaking stuff. I'm having a baby. On my own. Don't worry about it. It's been happening since the beginning of time and women have dealt with it, just as I am. So…' She tilted her chin up with a fierce gesture of pride and a bright strand of hair came tumbling down to lie against one freckled cheek. 'Was there anything else?'

Niccolò shook his head with frustration. Was she playing games? Did she really think that, having tracked her down, he was going to walk out of her life again and act as if nothing had happened? 'You think I'm just going to renege on my responsibilities?' he demanded roughly. 'That I would leave the mother of my child to continue working as a servant?'

'There's nothing wrong with being a housekeeper,' she defended hotly. 'Certainly nothing to be ashamed of.'

'No?' His voice grew silky. 'So why, I wonder, did you keep that rather significant fact hidden from me?'

Lizzie chewed on her lip as she wondered how to answer him. If their passionate liaison had continued a bit longer—she might have confided that she had enjoyed being someone else for once. A woman able to make a gorgeous man regard her with hunger and passion in his eyes, rather than being treated as invisible, or part of the furniture. A woman who had felt like a gorgeous man's equal for once. But if she told him that *now*, wouldn't it indicate that her self-esteem had been at an all-time low? Which wouldn't do much for her morale. It would make her appear weak and she needed to be strong, for all kinds of reasons—but mostly for the sake of her baby.

'I didn't tell you any lies,' she said.

'No, you didn't. But you let me think—'

'What? That I was posh? That I was rich? Why, are those the only sort of women you have sex with, Niccolò?'

'I hadn't had sex for over a year before that afternoon,' he gritted back.

Lizzie wasn't sure why this unexpected confidence gave her a huge rush of pleasure, only that it did. It slugged through her veins like honey and made her feel as if she were lying in a warm bath. But that type of reaction was dangerous. It belonged to someone attempting to read too much into a situation which Niccolò Macario clearly regretted.

'You made an assumption about who I really was, based on my appearance,' she said coolly. 'I'd tried on one of Sylvie's designer dresses because she owed me money and didn't have it. She told me I could sell some of the pieces online and that's what I was planning to do. So instead of being in my frumpy old grey dress, I was wearing designer for the first time in my life. You obviously thought I was someone completely different when I opened the door, and I was having far too much fun to correct you.'

'I see. And were you aware of *my* identity?' he questioned, with equal cool. 'Before I arrived?'

'Well, yes. Of course I was. Sylvie told me you were expected and the estate agent had already rung me up that morning'. She stared at him, unsure of where the conversation was heading until the inference behind his drawled question become insultingly clear. 'Hang on a minute. You don't think… You don't think I *planned* this? That I targeted you and had sex with you and gave you my virginity because you happen to be one of the richest men in the world?' She blinked. 'Maybe that I was even trying to get myself pregnant, so I'd have a meal ticket for the rest of my life?'

'I don't know. Were you? You might have been looking for the richest possible baby-father.' He shrugged. 'These things happen. Read the newspapers if you don't believe me.'

He didn't even have the grace to look apologetic, Lizzie thought furiously. And even though what he said might be true, it hurt like crazy that he considered her capable of such a thing. Though maybe she only had herself to blame. If she'd gone out to dinner with him first, would he have thought more of her? *Stop it*, she urged herself. You don't have to wear the mantle of blame just because you let passion run away with you for the first time in your life.

But at least he had done her a favour, by re-vealing his true colours. During weak, scary moments—often in the middle of the night when she had felt so lonely and vulnerable—she had sometimes found her thoughts straying to him. To the jet-black gleam of his eyes and the way he had made her feel when he'd held her in his arms and kissed her. That night he had made her feel safe as well as desired—particularly when they had shared a bath together and he had lathered her breasts with soap and washed her clean. That had seemed almost as intimate as having sex with him, and those kinds of memories inevitably prompted the occasional fantasy—which usually involved Niccolò turning up unannounced and telling her that letting her go had been the biggest mistake of his life.

Well, the first part of her fantasy had come true—but the ending couldn't have been more dif-ferent. Or more cruel. It seemed he was here to do nothing but mock her and hold her to account. *So get rid of him before your defences crumble and you dissolve into a mess of snotty tears in front of him.* That *wouldn't* be a good lasting memory.

'I'm afraid you credit me with far more devious-ness than I'm capable of,' she remarked. 'And since your wealth obviously makes you so mistrustful of other people's motives, then I feel sorry for you.'

'You?' he echoed incredulously. 'Feel sorry for *me*?'

'Oh, dear.' She tilted her head to one side. 'You don't think a humble housekeeper has the right to feel sympathy for such a powerful man as yourself?'

His jaw clenched. 'I'm not getting into a debate about status. This is just wasting time.'

'I agree,' she said airily. 'And since I've got a stack of shirts waiting which aren't going to iron themselves, why don't you let me get on?'

'Lizzie!' he flared, exasperatedly.

And that was her undoing. Hearing her name on his lips again brought back all kinds of erotic memories. Hadn't he whispered it just before he'd entered her—even if the word had frozen in his throat once he had broken through her tightness? Hadn't he murmured it again when they'd been in the bath together—and then later, when she'd served him up her trademark soufflé omelette, which had been the best he'd ever eaten, he had confided on a note of surprise. She felt her heart tighten and her voice was husky. 'My boss will be back any minute and it's better she doesn't find you here.'

His voice grew hard and steely. 'Does she know the identity of your child's father?'

'I haven't been using your name as a badge of honour, if that's what you think.' Her gaze slid to the shiny face of the bronze kitchen wall clock and she felt the quick thump of fear, because the last thing she wanted was to be discovered alone with the powerful billionaire. Imagine all the questions she'd have to answer.

How did you say you met him?

You were wearing your boss's *dress*?

'I think you've said everything you need to say,' she added quickly. 'So you'd better go.'

'But that's where you're wrong, Lizzie. I haven't even begun.' His tone was deceptively soft, because his black eyes were capturing her like a dangerous snare. 'And since you've made it clear we can't talk here, I suggest you meet me for lunch.'

But it wasn't a suggestion, it was more of a command. The words of a man used to getting his own way. And although prolonging this torture of seeing him again was the last thing Lizzie wanted, what could she do but agree? He *was* technically the baby's father—she could hardly pretend he didn't matter. But what exactly did he want from her, and why was her heart still racing? Was it because his power was so much greater than hers and she was nervous how he might choose to use it, or because she remained achingly aware of his physical presence, no matter how much she might wish otherwise? He was a difficult man to ignore. Raw energy radiated from his muscular body. His raven hair gleamed in the pale, wintry light which filtered in through the basement window. His eyes looked like glittering jet, set in the luminescence of his olive skin.

'Oh, very well,' she said, trying to convey a reluctance she didn't feel. 'If you insist. There's a café at the end of the road, just inside the park entrance. I'll see you in there, as close to two o'clock as I can manage.'

He nodded but his next words surprised her.

'Just make sure you put a sweater on first, will you?' he said gruffly. 'It's cold outside.'

He turned away and Lizzie was glad because her eyes had started pricking with the hint of tears, and she bit down on her lip. She didn't want him to be *kind* to her. She wasn't sure she could cope with that. Much better he be judgemental and disapproving. At least that would help keep her feelings in check.

Shutting the door behind him, she leaned against it and closed her eyes.

She'd already had her head turned by a black-eyed man with a killer kiss and dangerous smile and look what had happened.

Her fingers strayed to the curve of her belly and lingered there.

From now on, she needed to be on her guard.

CHAPTER FOUR

THE GLASSHOUSE CAFÉ sat within a grove of leafless winter trees and Niccolò positioned himself directly in front of the park gates, so that he would see Lizzie when she finally appeared.

If she appeared.

He glanced again at his watch, because it was easier to concentrate on logistics rather than the tumult of unfamiliar emotions he was doing his best to block. Was it possible that the petite housekeeper had stood him up? It was already a quarter off three and never had he waited so long for someone to arrive. His mouth hardened. Especially not a woman. It went with the territory of being a billionaire. Everyone was always punctual—in fact, people invariably arrived too early. They waited for him and hung onto his every word and jostled for his attention. It meant he never had to try very hard socially—others were always more than willing to do the work for him. But Lizzie hadn't reacted that way. He remembered the accusations she had flung at him and frowned. Had his wealth really made him so remote and inaccessible that the mother of his child had been unable to get an appointment to see him?

The mother of his child.

The phrase was cloaked with an intimacy which set his teeth on edge. It made his heart ache with hard-wired pain. It made the mantle of guilt even heavier.

His thoughts were interrupted by the sight of Lizzie, walking through a giant wrought-iron arch towards the café, tiny and instantly recognisable, her hair banner-bright against the gunmetal-grey of the sky. As she pushed open the door and approached his table he noticed that her thin overcoat barely fastened over the curve of her belly and a fierce rush of something he didn't recognise made him want to fix that. To swathe her in layers of cashmere and remove that pinched and suspicious expression from her face.

She spotted him instantly but didn't smile or nod in recognition. As he rose to his feet to greet her all he could see was wariness cloaking her features and making her regard him with undisguised suspicion.

'Hi,' she said, and as she removed the thin coat and hung it on the back of the chair, he ran his gaze over her critically.

She had changed out of the ugly tabard into a dress of sturdy brown corduroy, which must have been chosen solely for its accommodatingly shape, rather than any attempt to look pretty. Yet despite her pallor and tired eyes, there was something intangibly appealing about her, which made Niccolò's pulse unexpectedly quicken. Was it the spill of pale red hair which pregnancy had made extra thick and glossy—or the extraordinary colour of her pistachio eyes, which made it so hard to tear his gaze away from her face? He found himself wondering what she might look like if she took a little care with her appearance.

'Sit down. Please,' he said—and, to his astonishment, found himself moving round the table to pull out a chair for her, as if he were an accommodating waiter.

'Thank you.'

Her narrow shoulders brushed against his fingertips as she slid into her seat and as Niccolò felt the jolt of instant physical connection he felt a lump invade his throat. So, that aspect of their relationship hadn't altered, he acknowledged unwillingly— uncertain whether to be intrigued or alarmed. Their physical chemistry remained as white-hot as ever. His voice was thick as he resumed his place and offered her a menu. 'What will you have to eat?'

'Nothing, thanks. Just herbal tea for me.'

He frowned. 'Have you had lunch already?'

'No,' she admitted, chewing the inside of her mouth.

'Then why are you so late?'

Lizzie hesitated. She didn't want to come over as some sort of victim, but that was how it would sound if she explained that Lady Cameron had needed a silk shirt ironed before she went out to play bridge that afternoon. Didn't matter that she was supposed to have been off duty. Or that there were dozens of similar items hanging neatly pressed in her employer's ginormous walk-in wardrobe. It had to be *that* one—and no, Lizzie couldn't possibly go off to meet her 'friend' until the task had been completed.

'I needed to finish up some work,' she said vaguely.

'You need to eat—especially in your condition.'

She glared at him as some of the stresses and strains of the past few months came bubbling up out of nowhere, though maybe that wasn't so surprising. Because if she couldn't vent her indignation to the man who'd actually put her in this position, who else *could* she sound off to? 'What is it about pregnancy which suddenly makes the whole world an expert on my welfare?' she demanded. 'I *should* be eating and I *should* be resting. Well, I'll be the one to decide what I should be doing, if it's all the same to you.'

'So you're not hungry?'

Unfortunately, her stomach chose that very moment to give a loud and very distracting rumble. Was it the mention of food which provoked it, or the tantalising waft of soup as a waitress carried a piled tray past their table?

'A bit,' she admitted reluctantly.

An expression of satisfaction flickered over his face, before it was replaced with one of resolution. 'I thought so,' he said, lifting his hand.

It was weird sitting back and watching him take charge—and equally weird to have someone taking care of *her*, for a change. With consummate ease Niccolò soon had two waitresses fussing around him and the chef himself bringing a basket of warm bread from the kitchen—which was something of an achievement for a place where the views were wonderful but the service usually atrocious.

Before too long, Lizzie was sitting in front of a steaming bowl of vegetable soup, accompanied by bread, a chunk of cheese and a sprig of juicy purple grapes. And then hunger took over and blotted out every other consideration. With a hungry moan, she started eating and for a couple of minutes forgot where she was and why she was there. She even forgot who was sitting opposite her, watching like a hawk as she scooped up the delicious broth, finally sitting back with a sigh of satisfaction as her spoon clattered into the empty bowl.

'Better?' he questioned softly.

'I suppose so,' she said grudgingly.

His lips curved into a smile, which managed to look triumphant and supremely sexy at the same time. And she didn't want him to smile like that. She didn't want him to smile at all, because it was making her heart thump in a way which wouldn't do her any good.

'So.' The smile had vanished and his gaze was boring into her, suddenly hard and cold and calculating. 'We need to discuss the future,' he said, pushing away his tiny espresso cup.

Lizzie was interested to know what he meant by the word 'we', but couldn't think of a way of asking which wouldn't make her come over as needy. So she didn't say anything, just continued to regard him in silence.

'Do you have parents who are ready to embrace their roles as grandparents?' he enquired tightly. 'Siblings who are eager to be uncles and aunts, perhaps?'

Lizzie shook her head. If he was hoping for a huge and supportive family network which would pick up his share of parental responsibility, he had picked the wrong woman. 'My mum and dad are both dead.'

'You're very young to be an orphan,' he said and the unexpectedness of this observation made Lizzie disclose stuff she hadn't been planning on telling him.

'My father died when I was a baby and my mother wasn't…she wasn't in the best health, so I had to spend a lot of time looking after her and that's the reason why my schooling was so sporadic. I don't have any siblings,' she rushed on, realising that any more sympathy might make her vulnerable and she couldn't afford to be any more vulnerable than she already was. And then, because he was the father of her baby and she realised she knew practically nothing about him either, curiosity got the better of her. 'What about you?'

She was unprepared for the tautening of his striking features, or the way his eyes suddenly became hard and bleak and empty. 'This isn't about me,' he snapped. 'It's about you. And the baby. And it seems you have nobody to support you—'

'I don't need anybody to support me.'

'No?' His eyes narrowed. 'So how are you intending to manage after the birth?'

It was a mantra Lizzie had repeated to herself many times over the past few months, mostly in an attempt to believe it. 'It will be fine. Society is a lot more accommodating than it used to be. My boss knows. Obviously.' With a self-conscious shrug, she glanced down at her bump. 'She says I can carry on working for her. She's even prepared to let me carry on living there during my maternity leave—in return for a few light housework duties when the baby's asleep.'

'"*A few light housework duties*"?' he echoed, his voice hardening. 'What's that supposed to mean?'

'It's pretty obvious what it means, Niccolò. It's

called housework. That's my job. Cooking. Ironing. Cleaning. Washing floors. Scrubbing loos. I expect there are people who take care of that side of your life for you and you probably don't even notice they're doing it. Am I right?' She met his obdurate stare and knew she needed to be strong. To keep at bay this overwhelming urge to reach out and touch him. To test if he was real, or just some gorgeous figment of her imagination. 'Anyway, it's nothing to do with you.'

'Are you serious?' He studied her closely for a moment, then nodded. 'Yes, I can see you are. This has everything to do with me—and you're missing the point, Lizzie.'

'The point being what?' Defensively, she crossed her arms over her chest and as his gaze was drawn to the frumpy bodice of her thrift-shop dress, she found herself wishing she'd been able to buy some pretty maternity clothes. With what? The paltry stash she was trying to save before the baby was born, for a 'rainy day'? For a dress she'd only be able to wear for a few short months? And surely she didn't think that whatever she wore would have made the slightest bit of difference. He had walked away from her. He didn't want her. 'Are you trying to tell me you care what happens to this baby?'

'Why else do you think I'm here?' he questioned coolly.

Lizzie was glad she was sitting down, not sure

she'd heard him properly. Yes, that had once been her fantasy, on that terrifying morning when she'd done two tests in quick succession and had allowed herself the wistful image of Niccolò Macario cradling his newborn. But that had been before she'd come up against all the roadblocks he'd put between them, ensuring she couldn't contact him, and the realisation that he'd never intended to see her again. She could cope with that—of course she could. The idea that a man like him had been attracted to her in the first place had always been difficult to get her head round. Yet now he was implying…what?

'I can't believe you want to be a father,' she croaked.

'You're right, I don't. Or rather, I never intended to be one. Fatherhood was never part of my game plan,' he added grimly. 'But since it seems I have no choice in the matter, I don't intend to turn my back on my responsibilities.'

'You mean…that you're offering financial help?' she questioned cautiously, because she couldn't think what else he meant.

'Is that what you'd like?'

She blinked at him. 'Erm—'

'New house? Nanny? Would that work?' he continued silkily.

'That's very…kind of you,' she said, though she was so busy wondering whether she'd want anyone else—like a nanny—being hands-on with her baby, that she wasn't really taking in his words.

'Perhaps you'd like a new car, too?'

This was taking generosity to a ridiculous level, she thought—when his sardonic expression informed her exactly what he was trying to do. Making out she was a greedy woman with her eye on the main chance! Just like earlier when he'd implied she'd only had sex with him because she'd known he was so rich. What must life be like if you were as cynical as Niccolò Macario? she wondered scornfully. So play him at his own game. 'Oh, yes, please,' she breathed, injecting her voice with an acquisitive note. 'And plenty of shiny baubles, too. Diamonds would be best. Rare, glittering diamonds which I could sell on the open market.'

There was a split second of a pause while he seemed to be taking her demands seriously and then, to her surprise and, yes, her consternation, he tipped his head back and started to laugh. It was, hands down, the sexiest laugh she had ever witnessed and Lizzie couldn't stop herself from reacting to it. She felt a distracting tug of heat. She felt her tummy tightening and gave silent thanks that her pinafore dress was bulky enough to conceal the unwanted hardening of her nipples as she shifted awkwardly on her chair.

'Ah, *cara*,' he murmured. 'Your ability to inject a little humour into this unwanted situation will go some way towards making it a little more...'

He seemed to have some difficulty selecting the next word. 'Agreeable,' he concluded eventually.

Lizzie regarded him suspiciously. 'I'm still not sure what you're getting at.'

'Think about it.'

'Sorry. No can do. I'm pregnant and my head's gone to mush. Some people call it "baby brain", though others think that's very rude.'

'Then let me spell it out for you so that there can be no misunderstanding.' There was a pause. 'You cannot carry on in your current role, working in that house.'

'Why not?'

He placed his hands flat on the wooden table and, annoyingly, Lizzie found her attention drawn to his long fingers, remembering how they'd whispered over her trembling thighs, before bringing her to that noisy orgasm in the broom cupboard. Her cheeks flushed, first with embarrassment and then with self-directed fury. Why was she thinking about that *now*, when she had successfully erased all such erotic memories for weeks?

'Why not?' he repeated thoughtfully. 'Well, I'm no expert, but you aren't exactly glowing, as pregnant woman are supposed to.'

'Oh, dear. I'm so sorry to have fallen short of your exacting standards. If you'd given me a bit more notice, I might have had time to apply some blusher!'

'I have also discovered a couple of things about

your employer,' he continued, 'who doesn't have a fantastic reputation when it comes to keeping staff. Now, I'm no lawyer but I do employ a lot of people and I know it's against the law to ask a woman to work during her maternity leave.'

'But she's giving me a room and board!'

'So what happens if she kicks you out because she doesn't like the sound of a crying baby? And within a few months, the baby will be crawling. How will you do your job then?'

'Then I'd have to look for another job. Obviously.'

'What? Going from door to door with a squalling infant in your arms?'

'I hate to disillusion you, Niccolò, but most people go through employment agencies these days.'

He shook his head. 'I'm afraid this is all very unsatisfactory.' He leaned back in his chair. 'And I cannot allow it to happen.'

'Excuse me?' she squeaked. Lizzie tried to sound outraged but that masterful note in his voice was unexpectedly comforting, and although some previously unknown aspect of her character was making her want to bask beneath all the implied power which backed up his statement, she forced herself to see sense. 'I don't know which century you imagine we're living in, Niccolò, but you can't just come barging into my life, demanding your rights!'

'But you aren't going to deny that I do *have* rights, as the father?'

This really wasn't what she had expected. She wanted to be fair and she wanted to be logical, but now she felt confused. 'Are you sure you want to claim them?' She stared at him frustratedly. 'Aren't I just a woman you had some regrettable sex with? A one-night stand which has resulted in consequences neither of us could have foreseen? I would have thought you'd be happy about me giving you a let-out clause.'

Niccolò flexed and unflexed his fingers but it made no difference to the tension which was tightening his body. He couldn't deny that her words were accurate. He had come here today, not because he'd *wanted* to, but because he'd been driven by a sense of duty he couldn't ignore. He had imagined she would fall in a grateful heap at his feet. That she would be charmed and relieved at his offer to take her out to lunch and would have sat there, waiting eagerly to see what he had to offer.

But she had done none of these things and her attitude had taken him by surprise. She'd made it clear that she considered their relationship to be firmly in the past, and was prepared to bring up their baby without his assistance. Her fierce independence should have allowed him to walk away, his guilt assuaged by giving her a generous settlement which would keep her and the baby comfortable for the rest of their lives. But guilt was hardwired into his nature. And it seemed that it had not been assuaged at all. Why else would he feel such a strong sense of concern for her welfare, and a reluctance to let her go it alone?

'You look tired and overworked, and I cannot allow that to continue.'

'So what are you going to do? Wave a magic wand?'

He studied her for a moment in silence.

'You're going to have to come to New York.'

She frowned. 'I don't understand.'

'That's where I'm based.'

'Right.' Calmly, she took a sip of water. 'But I'm still not with you.'

'You must come and live with me.'

Now he had a reaction. She sat up straight, her soft lips falling open.

'*Live* with you?'

He wondered why he had put it so baldly—without nuance—knowing the tendency of women to read too much into a few simple words. 'Not *with* me,' he clarified abruptly. 'I'm offering you temporary shelter, that's all. A holiday, if you like. I will provide warmth, food and a generous expense account—as well as the finest medical care in the country—while you decide what you want to do.'

'No expense spared for the baby, you mean?' she questioned quietly.

'Why not?' he drawled, on familiar territory

now, as the conversation shifted into financial negotiation. 'I'm a wealthy man, with no dependants. Until now. I have more than enough for my charities to benefit from my fortune, so why would I leave out my own flesh and blood?' He leaned forward across the table, his voice low. 'Don't you realise I'm in a position to offer this child the best of everything?'

Except love, thought Lizzie desperately. All the money in the world couldn't buy that. She looked into his face, but as her gaze rested on the sculpted slash of his features, she could see nothing but coldness and calculation in his eyes. Every instinct she possessed was urging her to reject his proposal. Quickly she corrected herself. No. This definitely wasn't a *proposal*. This was an expedient offer from a powerful man whose motives were unclear.

Unlike hers.

Over the last few months, she had thought of this baby as hers and hers alone. She had become territorial about the new life growing inside her, which had allowed her to feel as if she was in control. If she accepted Niccolò's offer, surely that control would slip away. He was already talking about their child as an acquisition—an heir to inherit some of his vast fortune. Where would that leave her? Penniless Lizzie Bailey, without a qualification to her name? Would he try to edge her out—to dazzle their offspring with all the things she could never provide?

She wanted to push back the chair and run out of the café and pretend this conversation had never happened. But that would be the action of a coward and something her conscience wouldn't allow.

Stop thinking about yourself.

Could she honestly deny their child this golden opportunity, just because her pride had been hurt and the man who had made her pregnant didn't want her?

She couldn't keep the stab of hope from her voice. 'Are you saying you want to be a proper father to this baby?'

'No, I'm not.' There was a pause. 'That's the last thing I want,' he said. 'Neither you nor this child deserve a man like me in your life, Lizzie. But I'm prepared to finance your future and give you time to think about what that future might be.'

'Why are you being so kind to me?'

'Not kind,' he corrected. 'I don't do kind. Let's just say it's a kind of thank you, for not having gone to the papers telling them how I'd deserted you. Possibly armed with a few naked photos you might have taken while I was asleep. It would have made a juicy story, don't you think? *Niccolò Macario dumps his baby-mama!*'

'Are you always this cynical?'

'Always,' he agreed acidly. 'I find that experience has made me that way.'

Lizzie stared into the hard glitter of his eyes. He was painting a harsh picture of what sort of a man he really was. He'd told her with brutal honesty that he didn't want a baby, but would support her financially. So far, so fair. But there was one thing he hadn't mentioned. The thing which had got them into this situation in the first place. The old Lizzie wouldn't have dreamed of bringing up such an intimate subject, but that innocent creature was part of the past. For her sake, and for her baby's sake—there was nothing to be gained from being coy.

'What about…sex?' she questioned.

'Sex?' he repeated, elevating his brows. 'Surely you're not *propositioning* me, Lizzie?'

'Of course I'm not!' she declared furiously. 'I just thought…'

'What? That I'm trying to lure you to the States because I want to pick up where we left off that crazy afternoon?' He gave a bitter laugh. 'Then let me assure you that your fears are unfounded, *cara*. I'm not that desperate.'

'Desperate?' she repeated furiously.

'You think I am turned on by a woman who looks at me as if I am the devil incarnate, even though she might be right? Believe me when I tell you that I have no intention of installing you in my bedroom, Lizzie. I prefer my women a little less prickly and a little less pregnant.' He gave a soft laugh. 'You will be quite safe from me.'

Safe? Suddenly, Lizzie didn't feel in the least bit safe, because even when he was being angry he was devastatingly attractive. He still made her want to sidle up close to him and present her lips to be kissed. Her breasts still ached to be touched by him. He represented danger on so many levels, yet she couldn't deny being tempted by his offer. The constant nag of worry about not having enough money would be removed in a stroke—and what was the worst that could happen? She could come back to England any time she liked—he was hardly going to keep her prisoner in New York, was he? But he needed to understand that the impetuous creature who had fallen into his arms that day hadn't been the real Lizzie Bailey. The real Lizzie was careful and responsible and weighed things up. She was decent and honest and didn't let people down.

'I'd like some time to think about it,' she said stiffly. 'I can't just leave my boss in the lurch. I'll need to give her notice.'

He shrugged, seemingly unimpressed by this demonstration of conscientiousness, withdrawing a thick cream card from his wallet and sliding it across the table. 'Suit yourself. Here are my details. My plane leaves tomorrow. Let me know if you're going to be on it. Do you want a lift somewhere now?'

'No, thanks. I'll walk.'

It was a relief to get away from the distracting

gleam of his eyes and walk back across the park, even though the cold wind was biting viciously into her cheeks and penetrating her inadequate coat. She had intended to speak to her boss when she returned from her bridge lesson, but Lady Cameron cut her short by demanding Lizzie bone and cook three chickens for an impromptu dinner party she was giving that evening.

Lizzie's heart plummeted. 'But I'm supposed to be off duty—'

'And?' A pointed glance swivelled to her belly. 'Aren't you lucky to have a job at all?'

Insecurity won out over any championing of employment rights and Lizzie nodded obediently, more out of habit than anything else. In the basement kitchen, she stood shivering with her hands deep in icy water and entrails, trying not to retch, and somehow managed to produce and serve a three-course supper, and tidy up afterwards. But despite a fatigue which seeped deep into her bones, her night was restless. As the pale gleam of the winter morning crept in through the thin curtains, she suddenly sat bolt upright in bed and looked around the attic room as if she were seeing it for the first time.

What was she *doing*? First Sylvie and now Lady Cameron—both of them treating her like dirt. She had told herself she needed to be strong from here on in, mostly for her baby's sake. So how many more times was she going to allow herself to be exploited by unscrupulous employers before she came to her senses?

After showering beneath a meagre trickle of water in the poky bathroom, she packed all her possessions into a single suitcase, took out her phone and punched out the number Niccolò had given her. The irony didn't escape her when he answered. All those fruitless attempts to contact him in the early days of her pregnancy, when she had come up against an impenetrable wall of security. But now? Now he picked up on the second ring, his velvety tones making a complicated series of reactions sizzle over her skin.

'Lizzie?'

'I'd like to come to New York. If the offer's still on.'

'When?'

She drew in a deep breath. 'You said your plane was leaving today.'

There was a pause and when he spoke his voice was silky. 'What changed your mind?'

Lizzie stared out of the tiny attic window at the bare treetops silhouetted against the pewter sky. She didn't want to tell him about the tiny ray of hope which had flickered into her heart in the middle of the night, because that was ill founded and sentimental and he wouldn't want to hear it. It might even be enough to make him change his mind and, suddenly, that was a prospect she couldn't bear to contemplate.

'Well, I haven't exactly been inundated with attractive offers,' she confided, as carelessly as she could. 'So it seemed a bit short-sighted to turn it down.'

'Bene.' He didn't bother to hide his satisfaction. 'I will send a car for you.'

CHAPTER FIVE

'I DON'T UNDERSTAND.' Her voice sounded bewildered. 'Why are we in a hotel?'

Their whistlestop tour concluded, Niccolò watched the tiny redhead slowly circumnavigate the vast reception area of his suite of rooms. As she walked over to one of the floor-to-ceiling windows and stared at the skyscraper view outside, he thought how small she seemed in these vast surroundings, and how vulnerable. When she turned to face him her eyes were wide, as if she was having difficulty adjusting to her new reality. That made two of them, he thought grimly, wondering whether he had taken leave of his senses when he had blurted out his offer to her back in London. 'Because this is where I live.'

As she shook her head, her pale red hair shimmered. 'You live in a hotel? Who *does* that?'

Words seemed to fail her as her gaze alighted on a glass coffee table on which stood a stack of rare books. She had removed her coat to reveal a dress which appeared to have been fashioned from a pair of old drapes and was slightly too small for her, so that it clung to her fecund curves. The new shape of her body was glaringly apparent in a way he hadn't really noticed back in England. The heavy breasts. The slightly widened hips. When she did that unconscious thing of fluttering her fingers against her belly, she seemed the embodiment of fertility. She was pregnant. Lushly and terrifyingly pregnant.

And he had made her that way.

She stuck out like a sore thumb in the sleek bachelor world he inhabited. The crew on his private jet had been unable to conceal their surprise when she'd arrived at the airfield, emerging from the limousine carrying nothing but a battered suitcase and wearing that thin coat straining over her bump. The hotel staff clearly thought the same— though Niccolò had glowered when he'd noticed one of the bellboys staring at her askance, before sending the hapless individual away without a tip.

Yet, for a man who always travelled solo, Lizzie Bailey had proved to be an undemanding companion during the flight from London to New York. There had been no mindless chatter, at which women excelled. Even the barrage of questions which he assumed that she of all people had the right to ask hadn't materialised. She had spotted one of the large bedrooms on board and—after establishing that, yes, of course she was allowed to use it—had shut herself away for much of the flight.

As they'd flown over the Atlantic, Niccolò kept glancing towards a door which had remained firmly closed. Like all powerful men, he was attracted to the things which seemed unavailable. Annoyingly, he'd found himself wondering whether she was sleeping naked and how that might look, then reminded himself that sex was a complication he definitely didn't need.

She hadn't emerged until shortly before landing, and despite his determination to subdue his desire, he had found himself focussing reluctantly on the bareness of her lips, fighting back a desire to take her in his arms and taste their honeyed softness again.

Yet now, seeing her rounded body silhouetted against the glittering Manhattan skyline, that desire had been replaced by incredulity, and yes, dread. Her presence was driving home the realisation that he had placed himself at the centre in a situation he'd always gone out of his way to avoid. His heart began to hammer painfully against his ribcage. Wouldn't a new baby bring back all the memories he'd worked so hard to suppress, haunting him with guilt and grief all over again?

He must not let it. He must compartmentalise—which he was good at—and put things in perspective. He had offered Lizzie Bailey nothing but a temporary refuge and once she realised the true extent of the funds he was willing to put at her disposal she would doubtless wish to return to her own country and cash in on them. To make a fresh start for herself and find a husband who was capable of giving her the affection she undoubtedly craved. He gave a small nod of satisfaction. People lived complicated lives these days—why should theirs be any different? Every dilemma had a solution if you searched for it hard enough.

'You don't approve of the accommodation?' he hazarded sarcastically. 'It is a little too cramped perhaps?'

'Ha-ha. Very funny. I can't believe there are actually...' she did a rapid calculation on her fingers '...six rooms! Six!'

Drawing in a deep breath, she redirected her verdant gaze at him and Niccolò was irritated by the corresponding ripple of pleasure that gave him.

'You could probably live in a palace if you wanted to,' she persisted. 'So why here?'

He shrugged. His usual response to a question he'd been asked countless times was that he owned the hotel, which was true. But flippancy seemed inappropriate in Lizzie's case and to talk about his many assets might be interpreted as boastful. She was pregnant with his child and somehow that uneasy realisation filled him with a responsibility to answer her questions honestly, and to expect the same honesty in return. Anything else would be a waste of his valuable time.

'I like to keep my life simple and this allows

me to do so,' he explained. 'I have all my needs catered to, with the minimum amount of involvement or effort on my part. Things are brought to me at the push of a button. There are constantly changing staff, whose names I never need bother learning.' He shrugged as his gaze flickered over to the panoramic wall of windows. 'As well as having one of the best views in the city—it suits me.'

'Yes, I get all that,' she said slowly. 'It just doesn't feel much like home, that's all.'

'That's intentional. Because I'm not looking for a home, Lizzie. My life is nomadic. I travel a great deal. I have a plane on permanent standby. I don't stay anywhere for very long. I don't have any emotional connections to places, the way that other people do.'

'Yet when you came to Ermecott Manor, you seemed to love it,' she observed.

'Let's not go overboard. Love isn't a word which tends to feature in my vocabulary.' He gave a short laugh. 'I liked it well enough.'

Her gaze grew thoughtful, as if she was storing away this nugget of information for future use—which was exactly what he intended she do.

'Yet you didn't put in an offer, did you?'

'No,' he agreed. 'I didn't.'

'Why was that?'

'Mmm?' he questioned distractedly because the skyscrapers outside the window were spangling her face with shafts of light, giving her skin a jewel-like luminance.

'You didn't think the house had potential?' she persisted.

'Oh, it had plenty of potential. It was one of the best properties of its kind to come on the market all year, and I thought very seriously about buying it.'

'But you changed your mind.' She glanced down and began to fiddle with the snug skirt of her floral dress, as if reluctant to meet his eye and when she lifted her face again, her cheeks were flushed. 'Did…did what happened with me influence your decision?'

Niccolò's eyes narrowed, surprised she'd had the guts to ask the question and risk the rejection she must have known was coming. But wasn't it better she realised exactly where she stood? If he explained it to her in stark shades of black and white, so there could be no grey areas of misunderstanding? 'In a sense, yes. It would have been difficult if we kept running into one another.'

'In case I formed an unwanted attachment towards you?'

'That was always a consideration,' he conceded.

'Because you're so irresistible?' She gave a short laugh. 'Because women find it so hard to forget you once you've had sex with them?'

Unapologetically, he shrugged. 'So they tell me.'

'That's the most big-headed thing I've ever heard!'

If she'd been a little more experienced he might have replied with mocking innuendo but no matter how he answered, he wasn't going to deny the truth. He was an excellent lover. He knew that. He prided himself on giving pleasure, as well as receiving it. But women often mistook good sex for something different, because they were programmed to search for something deeper and he was programmed to avoid exactly that. Occasionally he embarked on a relationship, but it was nearly always brief and he was always strangely relieved when it ended and he could feel free once more. He knew his limitations. He was too complicated and emotionally repressed for any kind of romantic partnership. Too damaged for anything permanent. That was the reason he only ever had liaisons with women who knew the score. Who regarded sex as an enjoyable pastime, not as some kind of audition to become his wife.

He'd thought Lizzie Bailey was cast from the same mould—with her foxy green dress and inviting eyes. Yet her unexpected innocence and sweet fervour had placed her in a category of her own, which had thrown him at the time. He'd spoken the truth when he'd said he wouldn't have gone near her if he'd known she was a virgin—though deep down he wondered whether he would have been strong enough to resist the allure she had radiated that day. His heart had been raw and aching on the anniversary of the deaths. He had been filled with sorrow and regret. Deep in emotional pain, she had been exactly what he needed at that time.

A transient and sensual balm for his troubled soul and nothing more.

The night which had followed had been sensational. Her lack of experience had meant that everything they'd done had been new to her and she had been the most delightful of students, eager to learn what pleased him and shyly discovering what gave *her* pleasure. The intensity of her many orgasms had been matched by his own—a mind-blowing amount—even by his standards.

But when he had woken next morning and seen her serene smile as she'd snuggled up to him, warning bells had sounded in his head. She had been too inviting. Too sweet and too soft. Her nipples like ripe cherries topping the creamy mounds of her breasts, he had wanted to lick her all over. He had wanted to thrust into her wet tightness again and again with a need which had threatened to devour him. But these days he was better equipped to recognise danger in its many forms, and these days he always heeded it. Ignoring the hard throb of an erection, he had forced himself to get out of bed and steel his heart against the confusion in her green eyes. He hadn't wanted to get to know her better, because there was no point. He hadn't wanted to hurt her.

'It just seemed less complicated to walk away,' he concluded heavily.

'So what made you walk back?'

There was a pause. 'Guilt,' he said eventually. 'And duty. Nothing more.'

'Wow. You don't pull any punches, do you?'

'I don't lead women on. Not even in your case. Especially in your case, Lizzie. You are carrying my child and because of that I owe you the truth. It's better you understand that I'm not planning to play happy families any time soon.' His mouth hardened. 'And I'm certainly not the man of your dreams.'

'Oh, I really don't need you to tell me that, Niccolò,' she said. 'I'd sort of worked that out for myself.'

Something about the quiet dignity of her response made him feel uncomfortable and, suddenly, he needed to get away. He glanced at his watch as if it were a lifeline. 'Look, I have a number of work calls I need to make before dinner, so why don't you—?'

'Make myself at home?' she interjected sarcastically.

'Meet me back here at seven,' he said, refusing to rise to the sudden fire in her eyes. To show her that he was in control, even if at that precise moment he didn't feel it. 'We can either eat dinner in the hotel restaurant or have something prepared here. Up to you.'

Lizzie hesitated. She didn't want to walk into a posh hotel restaurant in her cheap clothes, but the thought of sitting at either end of a table which could comfortably have seated ten in Niccolò's private dining room filled her with horror. There had been too many high-end new experiences to contend with today and she figured she had just about reached her limit.

'If you want something fancy, then please go ahead without me. I certainly don't mind if you want to go out on your own,' she said. 'I'd be perfectly happy staying in with a sandwich.'

His lips curved into a reluctant smile. 'I think the chef could just about run to that.'

'I'm perfectly capable of making it myself.'

'I'm sure you are.' There was a pause. 'But the staff get a little proprietorial about the kitchen. Perhaps you can relate to that?'

'Are you trying to reinforce my servant status?' she demanded.

'Not at all.' He held up his palms in mock appeal. 'I was simply being factual.'

His contrition seemed genuine but Lizzie didn't trust herself to say another word as she left the room and made her way to the accommodation he'd pointed out to her a few minutes ago. It was difficult to take in just how arrogant he could be. All that stuff about women finding him irresistible—what an ego!

But you found him irresistible, didn't you? taunted the voice of her conscience. *You let him have sex with you within an hour of meeting.*

She had gasped out her disbelieving pleasure

in a broom-cupboard and then led him upstairs to bed. She had behaved in a way she hadn't thought herself capable of and the worst thing was that she didn't seem to have moved on from that position.

She shut her bedroom door, barely registering the enormous room or clever lighting, which made the whole place glow like a carefully staged department-store window. The expensive furniture in the adjoining sitting room was equally wasted on her because all she could see was the bed, looming up like a great monolith. The biggest bed she had ever seen. The snowy linen seemed to mock her and she found herself wondering why she had come here, and what she'd thought might happen. The practical aspects of accepting Niccolò's offer had made perfect sense but she saw now that she had been naïve about the emotional ones. Had she imagined she would suddenly acquire a miraculous immunity to his sizzling sex appeal? Or that he might override his terse assurance that he wouldn't be inviting her to share his bedroom? Because, given the current way she was feeling, she would find that very difficult to turn down.

It had never even occurred to her that she would react like this, even though she'd read plenty of books full of advice for pregnant women. They'd said that sexual desire was perfectly normal when you were expecting a baby, but she'd thought that had been aimed at prospective parents who were in a loving and committed relationship. Living with

a man who had gone out of his way to cut you out
of his life should have been enough to have killed
her desire for him stone-dead. But nobody could
predict what would happen until you were actually
in the situation yourself. And the truth was that she
still wanted him. Despite his overriding arrogance
and egotism, deep down she wanted him to sweep
her into his arms and make her tremble again.

How stupid was that?

Very stupid indeed.

Clicking open her case, she stared at her paints
and brushes and thought how long it had been
since she'd had a chance to use them, but her pregnancy had pushed all thoughts of painting dogs
out of her mind. After she'd placed them neatly
on the dressing table, she surveyed the remaining
contents of her suitcase with a gloomy eye. It was
disconcerting how out of place she felt in these
luxurious surroundings, in the thrift-store outfits
she'd accumulated. Like a muddy boot dropped
onto a white carpet. Everything was sparkly clean
and she felt dingy and faded in comparison. Scoot-
ing off to the en-suite bathroom, she turned on the
taps and squirted in some geranium-scented oil
before stripping off her clothes.

Unfortunately, her reflection bounced back at
her from every available wall as she waited for
the giant tub to fill. It was the first time she'd
viewed her naked pregnant body in a full-length
mirror—there had only been a tiny one in her attic

room at Lady Cameron's—and Lizzie was unable to hold back her instinctive flinch when she saw herself. Her petite frame was dominated by the curve of her belly, making her limbs look positively scrawny in comparison. Her breasts were big and swollen—the nipples two large, dark rosy discs—and surely her hips were far curvier than they used to be. It was a sobering vision to witness the physicality of her condition and see how much she had changed.

How shocked Niccolò Macario must have been to see her like this when he'd turned up the other day. He'd only had sex with her because she'd been dressed like a toff and had been giving him the green light in her borrowed designer dress. It had been a moment of madness and one which he clearly regretted.

But he was doing the right thing by her, wasn't he? He had offered her shelter. He had flown her to America on his private jet and installed her in a penthouse suite which probably cost more per month than most people paid for their accommodation in an entire year. He'd made an offer it would have been insane to turn down, but she needed to keep it real. She had been right to ask the difficult questions, even if the answers had been difficult to hear. And that was what she must continue to do. To confront the truth, no matter how painful.

Gingerly, she lowered her heavy body into the scented water and spent ages soaking in it, and for the first time in a long time, she felt properly relaxed. Afterwards, she blow-dried her newly washed hair and wondered what she should wear for dinner. Not that there was a lot of choice. But though second-hand maternity clothes were often frumpy, at least they never got worn much. The dress she pulled out was floaty and black with tiny gold stars embroidered over it. Best of all—it looked almost new. And although she convinced herself that there was no need to make an effort with a man who had stated emphatically that he no longer found her attractive, she still had *some* feminine pride. So she buffed up her ancient boots, then brushed her hair until it gleamed.

When she walked into the main reception room Niccolò was talking on the phone, his back to her, and for a moment she stared at him, her gaze drinking him in. Against the bright skyscraper backdrop he looked so tall and muscular and his black hair was ruffled—as if he'd been running frantic fingers through it. Yet despite all his wealth and power, which should have made him comfortable in such sumptuous surroundings, there was a strange restlessness about him. She was reminded of an animal she'd once seen at the zoo, before the laws had been changed. A snow leopard, pacing a too-small compound—all that untapped energy failing to cover a deep, underlying sense of sorrow. A caged beast behaving in that way was understandable, but what gave Niccolò Macario such a tangible aura of melancholy? she wondered.

He must have heard her because he turned and his reaction drove every concerned thought straight from her mind as he stared at her, the phone still clamped to his ear. She had tried to dress up to make herself look pretty but it seemed she had fallen at the first hurdle. He was diplomatic enough to try to conceal it, but Lizzie couldn't miss the flare of disbelief which sparked from his narrowed eyes. And suddenly she saw herself as he must see her. A pregnant woman in a cheap, second-hand dress with a pair of old boots which had been polished to within an inch of their life.

Suddenly, he seemed to remember that he was still in the middle of a phone call, because he started speaking. 'I'll have to get back to you, Donna. Yeah. Sure. I will.'

And in a funny sort of way, Lizzie wondered whether she should be grateful to Donna for bringing her to her senses. Whoever Donna was. His latest lover? Why not? He might have been celibate for a year before he'd ravished her in the broom cupboard—maybe that had been why—but there was no reason why he hadn't started putting himself out there again, making up for lost time. And if that was the case, that was one more thing she needed to accept. And she would do it.

She could do anything she set out to do.

'Hi,' she said briskly. 'Hope I'm not late.'

'No, you're not late.' He raised his dark brows. 'Find everything you needed?'

'Put it this way, I certainly won't be making any complaints to the management,' she said with a feeble attempt at humour, but he didn't raise a smile.

'Shall we go and sit down? We need to talk.'

It was another cool command. He pointed to one of the sofas—a long, low affair, sprinkled with velvet cushions which looked squashy and inviting and Lizzie sank down on it, grateful to take the weight off legs which had become suddenly unsteady. But then he sat down beside her and any sense of stability quickly deserted her.

She wondered if he knew how he was making her feel, just by being this close. Was he aware that her nipples were tightening and all she could think about was the way his tongue had explored their puckered flesh until she had yelped with pleasure? And then the way he had continued to lick his way down over her belly until—shockingly and deliciously—he had reached her thighs, which had parted so eagerly, as if having his face between her legs were the most natural thing in the world. But she didn't want to remember that. She didn't want erotic recall to play tricks with her mind and make her grow flushed and restless. It was inappropriate and it was dangerous, too.

'So.' She turned her head to fix him with a questioning look. 'What are we going to talk about? The sandwich filling on tonight's menu?'

'Practicalities,' he said succinctly.

Of course. 'Such as?'

He shrugged. 'You need to think about how you're going to spend your days while you're here. Obviously, you will see an obstetrician. There's someone at Lenox Hill Hospital who's been highly recommended, which the wives of several of my friends have used. I can arrange to have someone drive you to the medical centre. My assistant is currently dealing with that.' He leaned back, tousled locks of blue-black hair brushing against the collar of his silk shirt. 'But I run a very big company and work long hours, so I'm afraid I won't be around much during the day.'

'Oh, I think I can just about cope with your absence, Niccolò,' she commented wryly. 'I've managed for all these years on my own. Actually.' She hesitated, as she thought about the exotically named tubes which were lined up beneath the mirror on her dressing table. 'I've brought my paints with me.'

His eyes narrowed. 'You're an artist?'

Suddenly Lizzie felt shy about accepting this particular accolade, as if the only thing she'd been good at was going to come over as pretty feeble in his high-octane world. 'Only a very amateur one,' she said quickly. 'I've never been to art school. But I enjoy dabbling.'

'What do you paint?'

'Portraits, mostly. Dog portraits,' she elaborated, in response to the sudden elevation of his brows.

'Dog portraits?' he elucidated slowly.

'There's no need to look like that. It's a growing trend for people to want a picture of their beloved pooch to keep for posterity. I like to meet the dog to get a sense of them but mostly work from photos. A bundle of fur curled up in a basket, or bounding across a field, chasing a ball.'

'Fascinating,' he said faintly, lifting a hand to stem her flow, as his interest in the painting of animals had now been exhausted. 'But we really ought to concentrate on what you're going to do in the evenings, while you're here.'

'I'm quite happy to read or watch telly.'

'I'm sure you are.' His cell phone started to ring but he switched it to silent. 'I have a busy diary, especially at this time of year. I receive lots of invitations and I see no reason why you shouldn't come along with me. Much better than staying home alone all the time, don't you think?'

Lizzie chewed on her lip, wondering if she could cope with accompanying him to glitzy events. But he did have a point. Wouldn't she drive herself mad if she was left staring at the walls, like a thrift-store princess in a gilded tower? 'Okay,' she said casually. 'I can probably cope with being your plus one.'

'Please don't feel you have to overdose on gratitude.'

'Don't worry, I won't.'

His gaze raked over her. 'You'll need some new clothes—'

'Nice, but not necessary,' she said tightly. 'I've got enough to see me through. Honestly. You've already been more than generous.'

'Poor but proud is an undeniably attractive combination in a woman, Lizzie,' he mused, his lips curving as he leaned towards her, as if to emphasise the point. 'Particularly when the sentiment appears genuine.'

Lizzie held her breath and her heart pounded. He was so *close*. So ridiculously and deliciously close.

His black eyes gleamed as he readjusted his position. 'But in this case, I'm afraid it will work against you. This is a wealthy city and the people I mix with are wealthier than most. If you don't look as if you fit in, you will feel even more of an outsider than you probably already do.'

'Wow.' She tried to lash out with sarcasm, aware that she really *had* wanted him to kiss her. 'You really *are* selling New York to me.'

'There's something else, too.' His eyes narrowed as he studied her. 'You're pregnant and you're living in my hotel suite.' There was a pause.

'And since I'm a man who is notoriously averse to sharing his space…people are bound to speculate.'

'And you're worried they're going to work it out for themselves?'

'I don't think you'd need to be a genius to make the obvious connection, do you? Which is why I think we should pre-empt the inevitable gossip and put it out there that it is…' there was a pause '…my child.'

Lizzie told herself that the possessive-sounding phrase didn't actually *mean* anything, but that wasn't true because it meant something to her, and she prayed her face didn't give anything away as she attempted to quash the sudden fierce aching in her heart. Just as she tried to block out the un-helpful image which his words had produced. Of a tiny black-haired baby, nestling against the bare chest of his daddy, just like in those fantasies she used to have about him before she'd taught herself they were too dangerous. She wondered what sort of father he might make, and wasn't there part of her which longed to find out? But he had never wanted a baby, she reminded herself.

He spelled that out for you in cruel, but help-fully candid words—he doesn't want to play happy families.

With an effort, she dragged her thoughts back to what he was saying. 'And then what?' she per-sisted, continuing on her mission to stick to the facts—no matter how painful. 'How are you planning to cope with the inevitable questions which will arise?'

'Why should there be any questions? We'll have told them everything they need to know.'

At this, she actually laughed. 'I think that's a bit naïve, Niccolò.'

Ebony eyes bored into her. '*You* are accusing *me* of naivety?'

She shrugged. 'People—especially women—will be desperate to hear the details about how we met and why you're about to become a father after all this time—especially since you're a self-confessed commitment-phobe. So, do we tell them it was a hook-up which started in the broom cupboard, or pretend our liaison lasted longer than a single night?'

His eyes narrowed into obsidian shards. 'Neither,' he answered silkily. 'If pressed, we say it was a short-lived affair which was over almost before it began and we are handling the outcome like two mature adults.' His lips pressed together in a cynical smile. 'A story is easy to kill with the truth.'

And the truth could kill, too, Lizzie thought, her heart clenching. It could destroy her foolish little hopes with a single, well-aimed blow. *It was over almost before it began.* His words, not hers. And they hurt. Why did they hurt so much?

'Fine,' she said flatly.

'There are already a couple of things in the

diary. A drinks party next week,' he said. 'That's what Donna was ringing about.'

'Who's Donna?'

'A friend.'

It was a word which carried a wealth of meaning—especially when you were pregnant and feeling ultra-sensitive—but the arrival of the chef bearing a large platter terminated the conversation. Which was probably a good thing. Much better to find out about Donna when she wasn't suffering from jet lag and was feeling more resilient. She lurched towards the pile of delicious-looking sandwiches. When it wasn't such an effort to pretend she didn't care if he was having a relationship with someone else.

Or to hide how badly she wanted him to kiss her.

CHAPTER SIX

LIZZIE'S NIGHT WAS punctuated with hot dreams of Niccolò kissing her, alternated with visions of giant silver sandwich platters and she woke late and slightly disorientated next morning, not quite sure where she was. She turned her head this way and that. Beside the bed was a remote control and one click made the blinds float silently upwards, like the curtain rising in a theatre. And there— in all its brash and glittering splendour—was the backdrop of the Manhattan skyline. She really *was* here. In the heart of New York. In a vast but slightly sterile hotel suite, in a hotel owned by the father of her child.

She spent a few minutes stretching expansively in the enormous bed, before making her way to the luxurious bathroom and experimenting with the different settings on the taps. Who knew that having a shower could be so complicated? After dressing in a pair of dungarees and a sweater, she set off in search of breakfast, but everything remained spookily quiet until she was startled by the sight of a smiling woman who appeared at the far end of the corridor, her white uniform making her look like a friendly ghost.

'Good morning!' she said cheerfully. 'I'm Kaylie. And you're Lizzie, right?'

'That's right. Good morning.' Lizzie's smile was bright but she was finding it hard to know how to react in this particular situation. She was there as a guest but deep down she felt more kinship with the maid who was walking towards her. What was the other woman thinking? she wondered. That it was bizarre to have this strange pregnant woman turning up out of nowhere, and installing herself in a separate bedroom in the billionaire's hotel suite? She swallowed, trying to reclaim some sense of identity. 'Erm… I wonder if you could point me in the direction of the kitchen? I was thinking I might make myself some breakfast.'

'Oh, don't you worry about that,' said Kaylie, with an airy wave of her hand. 'I'll bring you whatever you fancy. How about eggs—any way you like? Or some pancakes? Chef does a mean pancake.'

'Pancakes would be great,' said Lizzie, feeling about twelve. Except that nobody had ever clucked around her like this, had they? Her mother had spent a lot of time in bed with her 'nerves', like a character from a Victorian novel. Treats had been in very short supply and they'd come either courtesy of schoolfriends, or hard won by Lizzie herself.

'Go and sit yourself down in the dining room and I'll bring it through,' said Kaylie. 'There's a letter in there waiting for you.'

Lizzie made her way into the dining room, which she'd rejected as too formal last night, so goodness only knew how it would feel this morning. But it was strange how your mood could lift in the cold, clear light of day. The room was hung with stunning oil paintings and there was a vase of flowers at the centre of the polished table, which were filling the room with the most delicate and delicious scent. And there, propped up against the crystal bowl of creamy roses was an envelope with distinctive black handwriting on the front, which Lizzie instinctively recognised as belonging to Niccolò.

She was right. The script was bold and slashing, the words succinct. But, despite the maid's description, it certainly wasn't long enough to qualify as a letter.

Lois, my assistant, will ring you after breakfast. Ask her for anything you need. N

There was no affection or softness in the brief message. But perhaps she should embrace his lack of guile, rather than despair of it. He wasn't pretending to feel anything for her, was he? He wasn't saying things he didn't mean, which meant he was fundamentally honest. Surely that would help curtail her foolish tendency to build fanciful dreams around him.

She ate the pancakes, which were delicious, and drank copious amounts of jasmine tea, and was just piling up her crockery when Kaylie appeared in the doorway, a telephone in her hand. Shaking her head in mock reprimand at Lizzie's attempts to clear up, she handed her the phone.

'Hello,' said Lizzie brightly, feeling the annoying sink of her heart when she heard a female voice she didn't recognise.

'Lizzie? This is Lois Kenton, Nic's assistant. He asked me to ring once you'd finished breakfast.'

'How do you know that? Do you have X-ray vision or something?' asked Lizzie, only half joking.

'No. Kaylie buzzed me over once you were done.' The other woman's voice was kind. 'I hope you're settling in okay?'

'Yes, it's…' Lizzie looked up, wondering now if there were spy cameras hidden in the ceiling '…very luxurious,' she finished truthfully.

'I'm glad. If there's anything you need, just holler. I've made an appointment at Lenox Hill Hospital tomorrow morning at eleven. Dr Campbell is one of the country's finest obstetricians and he comes highly recommended. I hope that's okay? One of my assistants, along with a car, will call to collect you at ten—because there will be paperwork to complete.'

'Th-thanks,' Lizzie said, feeling slightly overwhelmed by all this smooth efficiency.

'I also understand that you're looking to update your wardrobe and we can help you with that, too.'

Lizzie started to bristle defensively until she reminded herself that Lois was only relaying what she'd been told by her boss. *Don't shoot the messenger.* 'I think I'll take a rain check on that one,' she said politely, until something occurred to her. 'Lois. I don't know if you can help, but I need something to do while I'm here and I… Well, I paint portraits of dogs and maybe you could ask around. To see if anyone is interested. Oil on canvas—though I need to get hold of some canvasses.'

'I can sort that out for you. And, as it happens, I know someone who would be very interested,' said Lois. 'Me!'

'Really?'

'Really.'

'What have you got?'

'A bichon frise! Called Blanche.'

'Oh! Lucky you. I love that breed. Could you get a few photos of her to me? And maybe a favourite toy. Doesn't matter if it's all chewed up, or has a bit missing. Just something particular to her, so that of all the bichon frises in the world, it could only be Blanche.'

'Sure,' said Lois. 'I'll bring something in and give it to Nic to pass on to you.'

The dog-friendly conversation continued in this vein for a couple more minutes, until finally Lizzie hung up, delighted to have got her first commission. And Lois had been very sweet, there was no denying that. She hadn't asked her any intrusive questions, had she? Perhaps this experience wasn't going to be the ordeal she'd anticipated. She just needed to get real. To accept Niccolò for the man he was, not the dream lover she wanted him to be.

But a couple of hours spent in the high-rise suite were enough to have her pacing the rooms restlessly. Didn't seem to matter how spacious the suite was—bottom line was that she was stuck at the very top of a steel and concrete box and she felt trapped. It seemed her fears of being stuck in a gilded tower weren't far off the mark. She tried watching TV, but, despite the biggest screen she had ever seen, she couldn't find anything she wanted to watch, and flicking through the channels made her even more restless.

She was used to being outside in her down time, and although the sky beyond the tall buildings was the colour of dark steel, Lizzie felt a sudden desire to be out in the fresh air, away from the carefully controlled temperature of the hotel suite. This might not be a *real* holiday, but this was the first time she hadn't worked in years, so why not make the most of it? She keyed in the Wi-Fi code on her phone, studied the map to see that Central Park was conveniently close and consulted the temperature. Cold. Very cold. She added a cardigan before putting on her coat, though the extra layer meant there was an even bigger gap at the front. Then she wound a scarf around her neck and set off for a walk, running into Kaylie in the entrance hall, who was arranging a burst of amber roses in a tall vase.

The maid's expression was one of unfeigned alarm as she took in Lizzie's state of dress.

'You're planning on going out somewhere?'

'Only for a walk,' said Lizzie, with a smile. 'It's such a beautiful day.' This was patently untrue, but didn't they always say beauty was in the eye of the beholder?

'But you don't know the city,' objected Kaylie.

'I soon will!'

Kaylie frowned. 'You don't want me to call one of Mr Macario's assistants?'

'No, honestly. I'll be fine. I wonder, is there a key I could take?'

The penthouse elevator was empty as Lizzie rode downstairs, but the foyer was full of the kind of people who looked as though they'd wandered straight out of Central Casting, all sharing the same common denominator of extreme wealth. Two towering men with the physique of basketball stars. Several beautifully dressed children who looked bored out of their skulls as they waited for their mother outside the hotel boutique. Hard-faced middle-aged men with their impossibly beautiful trophy wives. It was hard to feel comfortable as she walked across the lobby.

Was she imagining the glances being slanted in her direction, and the unmistakable sense of surprise which followed? No, of course she wasn't. Places like this were all about pecking order and it was obvious to anyone that she was right at the bottom of the pile. But Lizzie brushed off her insecurities as she stepped out onto the busy sidewalk, the cold air hitting her like a blade and so bitter that she almost turned back and might have done, if it didn't involve walking back through the foyer and risking looking like a fool. Besides, the thought of kicking her heels in that sterile suite didn't exactly appeal.

The car-crammed streets were busy, the air filled with the sound of a cacophony of horns—but seeing the yellow taxis gave her an almost childlike thrill of pleasure. The pavements were busy, too, and everyone looked so purposeful and confident. Everyone in a hurry.

With the aid of her phone she found Central Park without too much trouble and soon was walking the paths and hugging her coat around her as she looked around. It was a place which was so familiar from various films that she felt as if she knew it well. Such a beautiful space to have within the heart of the bustling metropolis, she thought as she glimpsed the distant shimmer of water. The trees were bare and, although they had their own kind of beauty, she thought how stunning the place would look in springtime and that thought stabbed at her heart. By spring, she would have a baby— and who knew what state her relationship with Niccolò would be in by then? Not that you could call it a relationship in any conventional sense of the word, which meant that normal rules didn't apply. What if they'd stopped speaking by springtime, if he'd cut her and the baby out of his life?

This gloomy progression of thoughts had pre-occupied her so much that she hadn't been paying attention to where she was going. At some point she must have left the main path to go off at a tangent and she quickly realised she didn't have a clue where she was. Retracing her steps only made it worse and her instinct was to stop a passer-by and to ask for directions—but she wasn't sure if it was her wild eyes or slightly scruffy appearance which made all the people she asked shake their heads and walk on. Maybe they were tourists themselves, she thought forgivingly, or maybe they didn't speak English.

She mustn't panic but she *was* panicking, especially as the odd flake of snow had started fluttering down from the pewter clouds, and she wondered what the chances were of getting totally stranded. What if the city was blanketed in a whiteout—did that kind of thing happen in New York, as well as in ski resorts?

If only she were the kind of person who could

read a compass—but what good would that do her when she didn't have one and wasn't sure which direction the hotel was in? Her heart had started racing and, inside her thin gloves, her fingers were beginning to feel like sticks of ice. Should she ring Niccolò? But how could she describe where she was when she didn't even know herself?

Her footsteps speeded up as she looked around, but she wasn't sure if she'd been in this bit before. That big bush looked familiar, but she couldn't be certain. She thought she heard a sound behind her and tried to reassure herself that no, of *course* she wasn't being followed—but that she shouldn't look round, just in case she was. And then, like her worst nightmare, she felt a hand on her shoulder and she sucked in a shudder of air. The hand spun her round, and she was about to scream when she found herself looking into a pair of familiar black eyes.

A pair of very angry black eyes.

His mouth was set in a furious line and a muscle was working furiously at his temple.

'Niccolò!' she gasped, instinctively reaching out to clutch his broad shoulders and she didn't think she'd ever been more pleased to see anyone in her life. He felt so warm and strong and safe that for a moment she just clung to him, like the proverbial limpet on the rock. He didn't say a single word for at least thirty seconds, but when he did his words sliced through the air like daggers.

'What…the…hell…' he snapped '…do you think you're up to, Lizzie?'

'What d-does it look like I'm up to? Is it such a terrible crime?' she demanded, her voice rising with slight hysteria. 'Can't I take a walk in the park when it suits me, or does my pregnancy somehow preclude me doing *that*, too?'

She saw him flinch at the P-word, but the anger still hadn't left his eyes.

His fingers dug into her upper arms. 'I thought—'

He swallowed the next word as if it had been poison.

'You thought what?'

'I thought I'd lost you!' he raged.

Taken aback by this unexpected blaze of emotion, Lizzie stared at him.

'Anything could have happened to you!' he continued. 'You're all alone in a strange city!'

'So are thousands of other people!'

'But not anyone as gauche and as woefully underdressed as you,' he gritted out, his gaze raking down over her coat, which was gaping wide open. 'I mean, come on—what the hell are you wearing, Lizzie?'

At least now she was on familiar ground and his caustic words gave Lizzie the strength to try and push him away and reassert her independence. But her balled fists felt puny against the muscular wall of his chest, and wasn't the truth that she liked being this close to him? Didn't she want to sink right into him and absorb all that strength and power?

'What does it look like? This is my winter coat,' she mumbled. 'Why don't you just go away if you're ashamed to be seen with me? Just because I c-can't compete with your f-fancy cashmere coat!' she said, her teeth beginning to chatter.

'This isn't about competition,' he negated. 'And it's nothing to do with me being ashamed of being seen with you.'

'Then, why…?' Her words died away as she stared at him. 'Niccolò! What are you doing?'

'Isn't it obvious?' he snapped, dislodging her hands and removing his dark overcoat, which he placed over her shoulders before starting to button it up. 'I'm trying to make you warm.'

She wanted to protest at this unexpected display of chivalry because he was standing there wearing nothing but a lightweight charcoal suit but, oh, the sensation of warmth from the all-enveloping coat felt like heaven and it smelt of him. 'You must be fr-freezing,' she breathed, choking a little as a gust of wind whipped a strand of hair straight into her mouth.

'Shh…' Niccolò found himself pulling the errant lock away from the cold tremble of her lips and smoothing it back into the thick fall of her hair. 'Don't worry about it. My car is waiting over there. Come on. We're going.'

And wasn't the craziest thing of all that he

wanted to put his lips where her hair had been and pull her into his arms and stand there kissing her, as if they'd been a couple of teenagers at the end of a first date? But he resisted the desire to touch her in any way, other than the protective arm he placed around her shoulder as he began to guide her along the path towards his limousine. He waited until she was ensconced beneath a rug on the back seat and he had turned the heating up, and the flakes of snow had begun to melt on her pale red hair, before giving voice to his concerns, careful to temper the full force of his anger and his fear.

'You can't just disappear like that in future, Lizzie,' he observed flatly. 'Without telling anyone where you're going.'

'I didn't think. I'm sorry. I certainly didn't mean to worry anyone.' She bit her lip but her green eyes were fixed on him. 'How did you find me?'

'I sent some of my staff to look for you.'

Her contrition of a few moments ago seemed to be forgotten, her voice rising with indignation as she glared at him.

'You sent some staff to *look* for me? I mean, what *is* it with you, Niccolò?' she demanded, not bothering to moderate her own anger, he noted wryly.

'Do you get off on spying on your housemates for no reason?' she continued furiously.

He leaned back to study the infinitely fascinating definition of her lips as they pursed together in exasperation. 'Point one, you are the first "house-mate" I've ever had,' he drawled. 'And if this kind of behaviour is anything to go by—you're likely to be the last.'

'Oh, yeah?' She elevated her brows. 'And point two is...?'

But her spiky challenge had altered the atmosphere and suddenly everything had changed. He felt a new kind of tension creep in and suddenly Niccolò felt close to helpless, because she looked so tiny and so alluring that all he wanted to do was to crawl underneath that rug with her.

She stared back at him, her eyes darkening, her lips parting, and the desire which fizzled through the air was off the scale. She wanted him to kiss her. He would have bet his entire fortune on that. And he wanted that, too. Hell, yes. He could never remember feeling such an overwhelming desire to kiss someone—except maybe in that damned broom cupboard. But even as his groin grew hard, he reminded himself that to act on his feelings would have consequences and he mustn't allow the needs of his body to tip them into an ill-judged relationship. He would end up hurting her and she, of all people, did not deserve to be hurt.

And neither did he. He thought about how he'd felt as he had run through the icy park to find her, logic deserting him as he'd imagined something bad happening to her. And he couldn't live with that. Not again.

He fixed her with a challenging look. 'Point two is that if I hadn't turned up when I did, you might very well have caught pneumonia.'

'Isn't that a little melodramatic?'

'Maybe. But it doesn't change the fact that you need new clothes,' he added. 'Clothes which are weather-appropriate and which actually fit you.' He knitted his brows together. 'So why don't you stop posturing about some pointless principle and make yourself an appointment at Saks?'

There was silence for a moment while she absorbed this and then she pulled a face. 'And what if I told you that it wasn't just some *pointless principle*?'

He met her gaze. 'Go on.'

'You seem to make out that just because you're offering to buy me a brand-new wardrobe, I should be falling over myself to thank you. Why? Is that what usually happens?'

'I've never bought a woman clothes before,' he snapped.

'Presumably because the women you usually mix with can afford to buy their own swish clothes, and that's okay. I understand why you're doing it, Niccolò and I don't deny that it's with all the best intentions, but I grew up with...'

'Grew up with what?' he said, curious in spite of himself as her words tailed away.

'My mother never really worked and we lived on benefits. Handouts from the state,' she filled in, as the American model was probably different. 'We did that because we had to, because she never tried to get herself a job, and she was okay with that. But it's not how I wanted to live my life and since she died and I've been on my own, I've never taken a penny from anyone.' She tilted her chin. 'I may not have had the most lucrative jobs in the world, but I've always paid my own way.'

'Which puts us at a bit of an *impasse*, doesn't it?' he observed slowly.

'I know. I can't even cook you meals to pay you back because you have a famous chef do that and I can't make beds or dust the suite, because I think it would put Kaylie's and all the other maids' noses out of joint. But…' her eyes narrowed considering '… I could do your portrait.'

'If you think I'm sitting still while you paint me, Lizzie Bailey, then you're deluded,' he told her softly.

'I usually do animals, but I think I could make an exception for you. Although come to think of it…' She tipped her head to one side and narrowed her eyes consideringly. 'Hmm. Yes. Definitely. I can see a distinct resemblance to an angry bear.'

And to Niccolò's surprise, he started laughing.

CHAPTER SEVEN

NICCOLÒ DROPPED HIS briefcase on the floor more loudly than he intended, the sudden rush of air causing the roses in a nearby vase to shiver. With impatient fingers, he began to unbutton his jacket, throwing it down on a chair with his usual attention to sartorial detail forgotten. He'd had yet another frustrating day at the office for reasons which were as inexplicable as they were irritating—and it was all down to her.

Lizzie.

Lizzie Bailey.

A freckled face swam into his mind as it had been doing on occasions too numerous to count. Pale green eyes and glowing skin. A pair of soft, rosy lips crying out to be kissed. He shook his head, but the image refused to budge and he scowled. Total preoccupation with his unexpected houseguest was now his new normal and he didn't like it. He didn't like it one bit.

For days, he had uncharacteristically found

himself glazing over during meetings at his company headquarters, in a way which had produced vague flutterings of surprise from his staff. Instead of focussing on the latest stratospheric profits of Macario Industries and finding new ways to increase them, which was what he was extremely good at—his attention had been dominated by one Lizzie Bailey.

He had tried too many times to analyse her allure—and this was the confusing thing, because he had dated women far more conventionally beautiful than her. But then, he'd never lived with a woman before and had perhaps underestimated the potency of proximity. He had deliberately placed her off limits, yet was discovering that the forbidden had a power all of its own. She was feisty and she was vulnerable—an undeniably distracting combination, made all the more affecting because he sensed it wasn't contrived. And then there was her air of stubborn independence. Her reluctance to accept any of his considerable wealth, despite being as poor as a church mouse.

But there were other things about her which were equally perplexing. How come she was so uncannily good at reading his mood—sensing whether he wanted to talk at breakfast time, or remain silent? Was that rooted in her experience of working as a housekeeper? But she isn't your employee, he reminded himself frustratedly. She was your lover—briefly—but not any more.

And wasn't that something else which was driving him crazy? Those vivid memories of how good it had been between them?

A muscle began to work at his temple. He had tried to deny, ignore, dismiss and subdue his desire for her—but nothing seemed to work. Punishing early-morning sessions at the gym had proved useless. Long hours at his desk didn't help. He felt as if he had temporarily ceded control to the tiny redhead, and since he was a man for whom control was key, this was disturbing. He'd even considered eradicating the pervasive memories of her curving body by taking another lover—although obviously, he would be very discreet about it. But although other women were always coming onto him and there was an abundance of suitable candidates from which to choose, he found the idea of having sex with anyone else abhorrent.

His mouth hardened.

He wanted her, and only her—despite the combative dialogue which sparked between them, like iron on flint.

He balled his hands into two exasperated fists.

There were a million reasons why he should be content to keep the pregnant housekeeper at arm's length, but when he sought to reassure himself by analysing them—they seemed meaningless.

And while he had been giving less than one hundred per cent at the office, Lizzie had been settling into her new life in Manhattan, according to various members of his staff who she seemed to have charmed into total compliance. Mostly, she had been visiting the city's art galleries, along with a guide she had grudgingly agreed to tolerate after the Central Park incident, and a security detail he'd arranged to keep an eye on her from a discreet distance.

Calculatingly, he had tried staying away from her as much as possible and had even stopped turning off his phone while eating dinner, which meant he was often able to distract himself with work calls instead of looking into her amazing eyes. But tonight he was taking her to a party and, weirdly, he was looking forward to it. It felt like a date when it most emphatically was not a date.

According to Lois, his assistant, Lizzie had finally capitulated and spent the day shopping at Saks, leaving the acquisition of a new wardrobe right up to the wire. He frowned. And that was another thing. He hadn't realised that Lois owned a dog and that Lizzie had started painting it, setting herself up in a box room within the apartment and making the whole place smell of oil paint. It was an entirely new—and unwanted—pattern for his usually frosty aide to arrive at the office bearing a clutch of photos featuring some tiny piece of fluff called Blanche and asking him if he could pass them on to Lizzie. He wasn't at all comfortable about his home life spilling over into his office life—but what could he do?

The hotel suite was quiet, which he liked, and the main reception area was empty, which he also liked. He gave a heavy sigh. It was at moments like this that he could almost imagine he'd got his old life back, and was just about to pour himself a restorative glass of whisky when Lizzie walked into the salon and Niccolò almost dropped the tumbler. He tried to scramble his thoughts into some kind of coherence because of *course* he recognised her—a pregnant red-head was hardly going to slip beneath anyone's radar—but he wasn't expecting such a visceral response to her dramatically altered appearance.

Gone were the ugly, shapeless clothes. She wore a fitted dress of ivory lace, which complemented her colouring and glowing skin. Her shiny hair had been styled into a fall of sleek waves which cascaded over her breasts and, quickly, he averted his gaze from their luscious swell. Reluctantly, his eyes strayed to her stomach and it was hard not to stare, because no longer was her condition concealed beneath a swag of shapeless material. Instead, in the close-fitting gown, her pregnant shape seemed almost to be *celebrated*. And wasn't there something daunting about that? His heart gave a powerful punch because he didn't like that feeling. So he focussed instead on her face… What had changed in her face? Niccolò regarded her suspiciously.

'Are you wearing make-up?'

She blinked, apparently surprised by his question—though he couldn't fail to notice the gleam of something unfamiliar in her green eyes, which looked a little like triumph.

'Just a touch. A little mascara. A brush of lip gloss,' she said, before slanting him a look of challenge. 'Why? Is that not allowed?'

'Of course it's allowed.' He reached for the carafe of Scotch, then thought better of it. 'You just look…different. That's all.'

'I thought that was the whole idea?'

'Yes, I know, but…'

Lizzie hid a smile as, for once, the powerful billionaire was lost for words. She might not have had much experience of men but even she could tell he was impressed by her appearance. More than impressed. For a moment she'd thought his eyes were going to pop out of his head when she'd walked into the room. And although that realisation gave her pleasure, it was superseded by an irritation that he was obviously so shallow. What did her mother used to say? *Fine feathers make a fine bird.*

He wasn't interested in the real her, she reminded herself. Only the dressed-up-doll version. First of all in the borrowed dress and now wearing a brand new maternity wardrobe accompanied by a series of jaw-dropping price tags, bought from a shop so dazzling that many times during that afternoon she'd wanted to pinch herself to check she wasn't dreaming.

But the dream was soon to become reality, because tonight Niccolò was taking her to some fancy cocktail party and although he had assured her that the Livingstones were 'good people'—whatever that meant—she was terrified of having to go out and face his inner circle. Galleries and hospital trips accompanied by one of his many staff were one thing. This felt very different.

'Remind me again why I'm going?' she said.

'Didn't we agree that it might make your time here more enjoyable?'

'Did we?'

'I'd hate people to think I was channelling Mr Rochester by locking you in the metaphorical attic,' he drawled. 'So why don't you leave me in peace and let me go and get dressed?'

Lizzie wanted to ask if he could please stop speaking to her in that voice, because the lazy intonation was doing dangerous things to her pulse rate. She preferred it when he was clipped and precise. When he was trying to avoid her. He was doing that for a good reason and she needed to heed it. She needed to stop melting whenever he was around and remind herself that he was unknowable and remote, and that was deliberate.

But he hadn't been so unknowable in the park the other day, had he—when he had found her wandering around in the snow? His face had been raw and savage, filled with a powerful emotion she didn't recognise. The usual gleam of his black eyes had been replaced by a bleakness which had chilled her to the bone and made her want to reach out to him. She had wanted to ask him what had caused it, but his jaw had been so set and forbidding that she hadn't dared.

In fact, she had contemplated the wisdom of accepting tonight's invitation at all, wondering if she was getting in deeper than she should by involving herself in his life like this. For someone like him, this was probably nothing but a mildly amusing exercise. He was powerful enough and wealthy enough not to care if he created something of a society scandal—in fact, it might even enhance his playboy reputation. Bringing a pregnant ex to a party was a pretty audacious move in anyone's books and it would probably serve her better if she refused to go.

But how would that come over? She couldn't hide herself away for the rest of her life, could she? Their night of passion might have been ill judged, but it had still been the most wonderful thing which had ever happened to her. Niccolò had made her feel things she hadn't thought possible. And yes, he'd done a runner afterwards and she had become pregnant as a result, which wouldn't have been on anyone's wish list, least of all hers. But from the first moment of discovering she was having a baby, Lizzie had been in a state of wonderment.

She thought about the lovely fatherly doctor

she'd seen at the plush clinic on the Upper East Side earlier that day who'd told her she was doing just fine—more than fine, she was positively *blooming*. He might have been a bit surprised but had passed no judgement when she'd explained that the father didn't want to be involved in any way, other than paying her medical expenses. She wondered what he'd say if he knew that Niccolò hadn't asked her a single question about the baby. She'd thought natural curiosity would lead him to enquire about the sex of their child, at least. But no. She wasn't even sure if he knew her due date. He didn't want to know because he didn't care, she reminded herself fiercely—and she was going to have to deal with that. She was going to love this baby enough for both of them. And she could. She would.

Climbing into the back of a chauffeur-driven limousine, Lizzie thought how incredible her new clothes felt. There was something to be said for the sensual feel of natural fibres against your skin. She'd bought new underwear, too—which she hadn't realised she needed, until the rather bossy woman in the lingerie department had informed her just how much her measurements had changed. Now, thanks to the delicately supportive bra, her breasts were pert rather than bouncy—something which hadn't escaped Niccolò's attention either— judging by the searing look he had subjected her to, before quickly averting his gaze. Her breasts had tightened and she'd felt a rush of pure lust in response. Did he realise that? Was he aware that he could reduce her to a quiver of need, with just a single smoky glance—or did all women react to him in that way?

The party was being held in a place called Tribeca, in a sprawling penthouse apartment at the top of an impressive old building, and from the moment Lizzie walked in, she was dazzled—because it was like being inside a giant snowball. Everything appeared to be white. White carpets. White sofas. A man in a snowy jacket was playing on a white baby grand piano. Against this stark backdrop, the guests stood out with dramatic elegance—the men in dark tuxedoes, and beautifully dressed women perching effortlessly on precariously high heels, their precious jewellery sparkling beneath the lights.

'Don't tense up,' instructed Niccolò softly.

'That's okay for you to say. You do this sort of thing all the time. I don't.'

'Would it help to tell you that you look amazing?'

She wanted to say it wasn't about how she looked, it was how she *felt*—which was totally out of her depth. But she wasn't going to flag up any more insecurities, especially not at a moment like this. 'Very kind of you to say so,' she answered.

'It's not kindness, Lizzie,' he said softly. 'It's the truth.'

'Don't be nice to me, Niccolò. It throws me off-balance.'

'Very funny.'

'I thought so.'

Everyone turned to look when they walked in. Of course they did. When you were a servant you noticed everything and Lizzie still thought of herself as essentially, a servant. She could see the women's gazes flick assessingly from Niccolò to her and then back again. What were they thinking? That they were a mismatched pair? Normally she would have agreed with them, but she was still glowing from his words of praise.

She scanned the room. There was a man with horn-rimmed glasses she'd definitely seen on a chat show back in England and, in a far corner of the penthouse, a leggy model with a Cleopatra hairstyle—surrounded by a clutch of adoring men. A woman in a shimmering gold cocktail dress and a mane of matching hair came gliding over to greet them. 'Nic!' she murmured, her smile brushing each of his chiselled cheeks as she leaned forward to kiss him. 'So good to see you.'

'Donna!' he responded, with a smile Lizzie had never seen him use before. 'I'd like you to meet Lizzie. Lizzie—this is Donna, our host.'

So *this* was Donna! His 'friend'—with all the possible permutations which that word carried. Lizzie gulped. She was so gorgeous, and so thin. And calling him Nic sounded incredibly inti-

mate, didn't it? As if she knew him really well.
She probably did. After all, *Lizzie* was the only
person in the room who knew practically nothing
about him, despite the fact that she was carrying
his baby. Why hadn't she bothered to interrogate
him and discover a few facts about the father of her
child before they ventured out like this in public?
It could be an emotional minefield if she was in-
terrogated by any of the guests and betrayed how
little she knew about him. She tried her best not to
feel intimidated but it wasn't easy because Donna
was everything she wasn't. Classy and rich and
confident. And nice. Really nice. This is the sort
of woman Niccolò should be with, not me, she
thought desperately. Until she reminded herself
that he wasn't actually *with* her, either. Oh, why
had she come?

'Pleased to meet you,' she said stiltedly.

'Oh, I *love* your accent!' purred Donna. 'And
the colour of your hair is adorable! What will you
have to drink, Lizzie?'

'Erm—'

'How about some soda?' prompted Niccolò.

'I'll have someone bring some over.' Donna
smiled, a quick flick of her fingers bringing a
handsome waiter gliding towards them. 'By the
way—Jackson Black is here, Nic, but not for long.
There's a big vote coming up and I know he's
desperate to speak to you before he goes back
to Washington.'

'Yeah.' Niccolò turned to scan the room before redirecting his gaze towards Lizzie. 'Would you mind? I need to talk a little shop. I won't be long.'

'No. I don't mind,' Lizzie ventured gamely, wondering if his departing squeeze of her arm was entirely necessary as he moved away. Because all it did was to remind her how little he'd touched her since he had reappeared in her life. She sighed. With him it had definitely been a case of feast or famine. She didn't think there was a centimetre of her skin he hadn't explored on the night she'd conceived his child—and since then nothing other than his dramatic intervention in the park.

And wasn't it insane how such a fleeting contact could make her react like this—making her dissolve from the outside in? Didn't it make her think about his hard body, next to hers? In hers. The way she'd husked out her satisfaction as he had been pulsing out his seed.

Her breath dried in her throat. *Why was she having such x-rated thoughts in the middle of this civilised social setting?*

With an effort, she tore her eyes away from his rugged profile to discover Donna regarding her with thoughtful eyes and she cobbled together a smile, aware that her cheeks had grown very pink.

'So, how are you finding New York, Lizzie?'

'I love it. It's so buzzy, and the service is great. Of course, it's still all very new to me,' she answered politely. 'I haven't been here long.'

'And this is your first trip, I believe?'

Lizzie nodded. *Say something. Don't just stand there like a lemon.* 'I was supposed to come here on a road trip,' she said truthfully. 'But then I split up with my boyfriend and it got cancelled.'

Donna nodded, her cool blue gaze directed towards her bump—and perhaps it was Lizzie's disclosure about her past which made her come out with a confidence of her own.

'I have to tell you, we were all pretty surprised when we heard about you, and the baby.' The glamorous blonde gave a soft laugh. 'So if you hear the sound of shattering—it's just the sound of a million female hearts being broken all over the city! Oh, please don't look like that, dear. Most of us are very happy that Nic has found somebody at last, we really are. He's been on his own for a long time, though not from the want of women trying to pin him down.' She slanted a complicit smile. 'Anyways, I mustn't keep you all to myself. Come and meet Matt, my husband.'

A completely inappropriate sense of relief washed over Lizzie, which briefly eclipsed her confusion that Donna seemed to be labouring under the illusion that she and Niccolò were a couple. 'Your...husband?' she managed, trying to distract herself, because now was not the time to fret about her hostess's words.

'Sure. We've been married nearly seven years

now. Nic was our best man, actually.' Donna's eyes twinkled. 'His speech was outrageous.'

'Hmm. Somehow I don't find that difficult to believe,' said Lizzie and this time her smile was genuine.

'Come on over and say hello,' said Donna. 'There are lots of folk here who want to meet you.'

Lizzie followed her hostess through the vast, bleached room as Donna introduced her to a blur of guests, including her handsome husband, Matt—who it turned out had been to college with Niccolò, in Massachusetts. In a way she was grateful it was a cocktail party and the common language was mostly small talk. If a select bunch of them had been gathered around a dinner table she might have had a tougher time of it, mostly because she was aware of being an imposter— especially since Donna wasn't the only one who made the assumption that she and Niccolò were an item. How shocked they would be to discover the truth, she thought ruefully. To realise that he hadn't asked her a single question about the baby he had never wanted.

But now wasn't the time to enlighten every person she spoke to and risk embarrassing them both. She just concentrated on asking lots of questions, because people liked nothing better than to talk about themselves. She was deep in conversation with a professor of archaeology, who was showing her a photo of his dachshund, when Niccolò returned. His shadow seemed to consume her as he moved to her side, as if he were determined to dominate all her senses with his presence, leaving no room for anyone else. And he was succeeding, because nobody else in the room seemed to have any real substance any more. Suddenly it was all about him.

His raw, masculine scent.

The power of his muscular body.

Those carved, patrician features.

That mocking smile.

The breath died in her throat. No matter how much she tried to convince herself that it was over between them, that didn't stop her wanting him and right now, the feeling was as powerful as it had ever been. Did he notice the instinctive shiver rippling over her skin and realise what had caused it? Was that why his black eyes grew hard and a sudden tension seemed to have crept into the atmosphere?

'Let's go,' he said softly.

'Isn't it a little early?'

'No.'

She thought how comfortable he seemed giving orders and how sometimes he behaved as if she were a puppet, whose strings he was pulling. Was that how the party guests saw her? As some passive, previously unknown conquest who had turned up at the party like a tame incubator and left meekly when the powerful billionaire commanded her to do so. But she smiled her way past the doorman and waited until they were back in the limousine and driving through the thronging streets of Manhattan, before turning to him.

'What exactly did you tell Donna about me?'

He turned towards her but the only thing she could see in the passing city lights was the glitter of his narrowed eyes. 'The facts, of course. That I met you in England and that you're pregnant.'

'And?'

He frowned. 'And what?'

'You were supposed to say it had been a brief fling and we were handling it like adults.'

'I did.'

'So why was she making out we had some kind of future together? Like we were...' Her words stumbled, but she forced herself to say them. 'If not exactly love's young dream, then certainly some kind of item.'

'Was she?'

'Yes, she was! Like I'd pretty much broken every heart of the women in this city.'

'That part could be accurate,' he mused.

'Niccolò!'

He breathed out an impatient sigh. 'I guess it's human nature to see the things you want to see, and she and Matt have been mounting a campaign for years to find me the *right* woman. A *good* woman.'

'And I suppose I couldn't be further from that

model, could I?' she retorted, aiming for brightness rather than bitterness as their limousine stopped in front of the hotel.

There was a pause before the chauffeur opened the car door. 'But there is no such woman, Lizzie,' he informed her softly. 'Not for a bastard like me.' His laugh was bitter as he guided her across the shiny lobby towards his private elevator. 'I just wish people would accept that.'

But despite the candour of his words, Niccolò's heart was hammering as the lift doors slid closed behind them, imprisoning them in this silent box, which was the last thing he needed. He'd spent the evening giving her space and that had been deliberate. He had tried to concentrate on what was being said to him, rather than watching her moving around the room, which had been his instinct. But now there was nowhere to look but at her and he couldn't seem to tear his eyes away.

Her hair was gleaming like fire beneath the overhead light and, in the pale lace dress, she looked soft and ripe and inviting. He could detect her scent—sharp as limes and sweet as blossom—and, vividly, it took him back to that night he'd spent in her arms. His blood thundered as he recalled the way she had given herself to him so fully. So completely and openly, and without condition. He remembered the exquisite feeling of tightness as he had broken through her hymen, and the sense of wonder in her voice when she had come that first time beneath his fingers.

He glanced up at the dial. Had time slowed, or something? They had now reached the fifteenth floor, with another eight to go and sweat had begun to bead his forehead, because this was claustrophobia with a spicy twist. Was she aware of the need which was pulsing through his body, and was it the same for her? Was that why she was staring at him like that—all startled green eyes, her freckles standing out like tiny stars beneath the harsh elevator lights?

'Lizzie,' he said urgently. That was all. But maybe his husky tone sparked something inside her because suddenly her lips were parting.

'Niccolò.' Their eyes locked. Her voice seemed almost slurred, though she'd drunk nothing stronger than water—and all he knew was that she sounded nothing like the innocent he had bedded back in the summer. Didn't look like her either, with that slumberous spark in her eyes and a soft smile curving her lips. Yet he didn't know how to be with her, even though his desire for her was off the scale. The rules were different. She was pregnant, for a start.

'Don't you know that you're driving me crazy?' he grated.

'In what way?' she enquired.

'Oh, no. You're not getting away with that, Lizzie. You're no longer qualified to play the in-

nocent,' he told her heatedly. 'You know damned
well what I mean. In every which way.'

'But you're the experienced one,' she pointed
out, her calm logic fuelling the fire of his senses.

'What does that have to do with anything?' he
growled.

'Well…' Her voice was soft. 'I have no idea
what to do in a situation like this.'

'You know something?' He gave a short laugh.
'Neither do I.'

Niccolò wasn't sure which of them moved first,
only that suddenly she was in his arms and he was
smoothing back her hair and bending his head to
kiss her, with an aching frustration building inside
him which made him feel like a novice. That first
touch was like wildfire—igniting all the pent-up
hunger which had been building inside him for
months—and he groaned as the tip of her tongue
entered his mouth, because never had such a simple gesture felt so intensely erotic. Why was that?
Because he could feel her fecund new shape pressing against him, terrifyingly unfamiliar to his usually experienced fingers?

Bitter thoughts attempted to assault his mind
but his body's needs were greater than the painful tug of his memories. Their mouths still locked,
he splayed his palms over her ripe breasts, luxu-
riating in their heavy firmness. He could feel the
diamond tips of her nipples pushing hard against
her lace dress and he wanted to peel it off and re-

veal her freckled flesh. He heard her groan as he deepened the kiss and now the scent of her cologne had been replaced by the far more evocative tang of feminine desire, obliterating any last vestiges of doubt in his mind. He wanted to ruck up her dress and feel her silken thighs. He wanted to touch her bud and feel it engorged with blood. But most of all, he wanted to be inside her again, with a wild and primitive hunger which took him by surprise. To fill her with his hardness. To hear her cry out his name, as she'd done before. To forget the world and all his memories.

He tore his lips away from hers as the elevator pinged to a halt and, although the doors opened, he stayed perfectly still and so did she. The tense silence punctured only by their laboured breathing, he dragged oxygen back into his lungs as he stared at her. 'I want you, Lizzie Bailey,' he said unsteadily.

'And I...well, I want you, too. I imagine that's pretty obvious.'

He gave a short laugh. 'Just a bit.' He could barely articulate his next words as the elevator doors closed again and still they hadn't got out. 'So, little Miss Redhead. What are we going to do about this?'

'This?'

'Do you want me to spell it out for you in words of one syllable?' he questioned huskily. 'Are we going to have sex, or not?'

Her cheeks grew even pinker, as if she were embarrassed by his choice of words, and that rush of colour made him realise exactly what he was asking of her. Suddenly, Niccolò was appalled at himself. Her sweet blush reminded him of her inexperience—not only around sex but, by definition, around men, too. It reminded him that he could offer her nothing but brief pleasure. No lasting commitment, nor even any lasting protection. Especially not protection. His heart twisted. Why the hell was he coming onto her like this, despite all those stern pronouncements he'd made about staying away? Wouldn't he be putting her in danger if they ended up making out—and here, of all places? In the damned *elevator*? Had he learned nothing at all, or did he still excel at making disastrous choices?

Breaking away from her, he felt the wash of self-contempt. 'This is *not* going to happen,' he stated angrily. 'We are not a couple. We were never intended to be. And if we start having sex, the boundaries are going to be blurred even more. For you, especially. Do you understand what I'm saying, Lizzie?'

Lizzie met his heated gaze, her natural indignation that he should speak to her in that rather patronising way blotted out by a keen sense of curiosity. She wanted to know what he'd meant when he'd stated he was a bastard earlier, in that flat and empty voice. She wanted to know what had caused that terrible look of anguish to tauten his sculpted features a minute ago. But how could she ask him when everything was complicated by her physical reaction to him? The tension between them was stretched so tight she suspected it would take very little to snap it. One move from her and she suspected he would be kissing her again and making her melt helplessly beneath the seeking pressure of his lips. And that could end with only one conclusion.

With an effort she pulled herself together, because maybe he was right. Maybe it was better this way. Donna had implied that women had always thrown themselves at him and although Lizzie couldn't blame them, she didn't intend being one of their number.

'I understand perfectly, Niccolò,' she answered calmly. 'If you don't want to, then we won't. It's not a problem—in fact, it's probably the most sensible outcome, if I stop to think about it. But now, if you don't mind, I think it's time I went to bed. It's getting a little…*heated* in here.'

His face was a picture of frustration and disbelief as she turned away, but suddenly Lizzie felt empowered by her actions as the elevator doors slid open once more. It wasn't what she wanted, but it was the right thing to do—and sometimes that was the best you could hope for. She knew he was watching her as she walked along the seemingly endless corridor and only once she had closed her

bedroom door behind her did she let out the breath
she hadn't realised she had been holding.

She stared into one of the mirrors, not-
ing the brightness of her eyes and her flushed
complexion—but besides the signs of sexual desire, the tilt of her chin was resolute and she allowed herself a small smile of satisfaction. She
might not have much money or prestige to her
name, but at least she still had her pride.

CHAPTER EIGHT

LIZZIE GOT VERY little rest that night, despite telling herself that not sleeping with Niccolò had been the best possible outcome. She lay tossing and turning and trying not to think about the man just along the corridor, but her unconscious mind was refusing to play ball. Every time sleep beckoned, the Italian's gleaming gaze and sensual lips kept flashing up behind her closed eyelids. She wondered how she would be feeling this morning if they *had* ended up in bed together. She wouldn't be filled with this aching sense of frustration, that was for sure.

She stared out of the windows at the night-time sky, which never really got dark in New York. Coming to America had seemed like the only sensible choice when Niccolò had made his offer, but it had always been a move fraught with danger. And the biggest danger was the way she felt about him. Still. She swallowed. It was relatively easy not to think about someone in a romantic sense when all you were doing was sharing the occasional meal, surrounded by swarms of staff—all eager to gain the billionaire's approbation. Less easy when you'd been kissing passionately in the lift and come within a hair's breadth of going back to one of the many rooms for a taste of the intimacy she'd been craving.

Staring at her phone, she saw it was still only three a.m., and sighed. It didn't seem to matter how much she told herself she shouldn't want the Italian billionaire after everything which had happened between them. The truth was that she did.

But, lest she try to delude herself, *he* had been the one to call a halt to it—using brutal words calculated to wound. He couldn't have made it plainer how he felt. *He didn't want his baby and he didn't want her, either.* That was the bottom line—and continually putting herself in the line of temptation was surely counter-productive. Wasn't it time to stop obsessing about Niccolò Macario and start focussing on what was best for her and the baby? She pulled the duvet up to her chin and snuggled beneath it. She needed to start thinking about going back to England and what she was planning to do when she got there. And that was a conversation the two of them needed to have some time very soon.

Eventually, she drifted off into a fitful sleep and it was gone nine when she awoke to a room which was unnaturally bright and she looked out of the window to see snow falling and big white flakes swirling down past the skyscrapers. The Manhattan skyline resembled one of those miniature snow globes you sometimes saw in museum shops, though when Lizzie peered out of the window on her way to the bathroom, she noticed that all the snow had all melted by the time it hit the pavement.

Tying her hair up and wrapping a scarf around it, she covered her dress with a smock she'd bought specially for working. The painting of Blanche was taking shape and she needed to finish it and give it to Lois before she went home. But it was the other portrait she was working on—a black and white drawing of Niccolò—which was infinitely more tempting. She'd never been so absorbed by one of her subjects before, her movements rapid and insistent, as if the pencil which stroked its way over the paper was a poor substitute for her finger.

She hurried along to the dining room, her appetite huge this morning. There had only been canapés at Donna and Matt's party and everyone knew they never filled you up. But as she sat down, it was a bit of a wake-up call to discover how quickly she had adapted to her new role as a rich man's guest, rather than as a person used to serving such a guest. It was remarkably easy to get used to plonking herself in a chair and telling somebody else what she'd like to eat, and breakfast had become her favourite meal. Often, Niccolò would be draining the last of his coffee when she appeared at the door of the dining room, his black hair still gleaming from the shower—sending out the erroneous illusion of intimacy and closeness.

But not today.

Today, the room was empty, save for Kaylie. How stupid that his absence could make her heart sink, even after everything he'd said to her last night.

Kaylie began to spoon out fresh fruit. 'Signor Macario left very early,' she announced. 'He said to tell you he's going to Pennsylvania. Would you like eggs?'

'No, thank you. Fruit will be fine,' answered Lizzie, shaking out her napkin and trying to do her blueberries and coconut whip justice, though she couldn't stop wondering why Niccolò had gone to Pennsylvania, or why he hadn't told her.

As soon as she'd finished eating she sought the distraction of work, in the small space she had made her own. She had been wrong when she'd counted six rooms in Niccolò's suite, because one morning she had stumbled across a box room—largely empty, except for a couple of suitcases. She had asked one of the porters to move them and reposition a desk there, so that it looked out over the city and was the loveliest workplace she had ever used. Best of all, it was north facing with a beautiful clear light and it wasn't long before she was lost in her growing portrait of the tiny white bichon frise.

After a lunchtime sandwich, she resumed painting, pleased with the shape it was taking, so deep in thought that she didn't hear the door open, or close again. She didn't hear anything until the sound of Niccolò's voice disturbed her.

'They told me I'd find you in here.'

She didn't turn round. She didn't dare. Her heart was hammering and her breathing had quickened and she didn't want him to see that. There was plenty she needed to say to him and she needed every bit of clarity and calmness she possessed in order to do so. 'Well, you've found me,' she remarked. 'I thought you were going to Pennsylvania.'

'I was. I rescheduled.'

'It wasn't important?'

'It can wait.'

'Right.' Still she didn't turn round, but now she could barely hold the paintbrush, her fingers were so clammy, and she knew she couldn't maintain this charade of polite conversation for much longer. 'Was there something in particular you wanted, Niccolò?'

He didn't answer, just walked across the bare floorboards to peer over her shoulder. Usually Lizzie hated it when people did that but her reaction was complicated by the fact that she liked him being this close to her.

'It's good,' he said steadily, his gaze flicking from canvas to photo. 'I've never met the dog, of course, but you seem to have created an uncanny likeness.'

'Thank you,' she said, wishing his praise didn't fill her with such a disproportionate amount of joy.

'You're welcome,' he said, but now his voice sounded strained. Different.

She turned round then, surprised to see the shadows beneath *his* eyes, as if sleep had eluded him, too. But she didn't comment on it, as she might have done if they were a real couple. Because they weren't, she reminded herself bitterly. Hadn't he drummed that into her over and over again?

Their relatively banal exchange was in danger of lulling her into a false state of security, but as she stared into the obsidian gleam of his eyes, Lizzie knew she couldn't let that happen.

So have the discussion now, she thought. *Don't wait for the 'right' moment, because there is no such thing. And don't use the image of a cute, fluffy dog to try to invoke some sort of emotion from this cold-hearted man because he doesn't seem capable of it.*

Rising from her chair, she rubbed her left hand in the small of her back and saw his eyes narrow.

'Are you okay?'

She wondered what he'd say if she mentioned that his baby was especially active today, whether that would elicit the kind of response she dreamed of. But she didn't enlighten him.

'I'm absolutely fine,' she said instead. 'But I'm thinking about going back to England sooner, rather than later.'

There was a pause.

'You said a month.'

'Did I?'

'You know you did,' he said heatedly.

'I don't remember signing a contract!'

She could see him dragging in a deep breath, as if she had taken him by surprise.

'Why?' he demanded. 'I mean, why now?'

'Isn't it obvious?' She stared at him. 'This isn't working, Niccolò, we both know that. I mean, it's working up to a point, but it's not ideal.'

'Is it because we didn't have sex last night?'

'No!' But his brutal candour cut through her defences. 'Well, maybe a bit. It's...' Be honest, she thought. Don't try to pretend to be someone else and then get trapped in a web of your own deceit. 'Staying here is doing my head in,' she admitted. 'It seemed like a good idea, back in England. I was tired and, yes, of course I was worried about the future, like anyone else in my position would be. And then you turned up like some knight in shining armour, and although you were grouchy you offered me a safe haven and a break from responsibility and it seemed too good an opportunity to miss. But that party last night was excruciating—'

'Every time I looked, you seemed to be enjoying yourself,' he mused.

Oh, you *stupid* man. 'I was. To an extent. They're a bunch of very interesting people, but I'm an imposter and nothing can take that away.'

'Yet Donna rang me up and wondered if we'd like to spend Thanksgiving with them.'

'Because it's *you* they want, not me,' she exploded. 'I'm not even your current piece of arm candy, am I, Niccolò? And I can't cope with the sustained curiosity which will arise if I continue to accompany you to these kinds of events. With me getting bigger with every day which passes while you...'

'While I what?' he prompted curiously as her words tailed off.

Was it so wrong to voice your worst fears? What did she have left to lose? 'I don't know,' she said slowly. 'I started thinking that maybe I'm providing some kind of hidden service in your life, which you haven't bothered telling me about.'

His eyebrows rose. 'Perhaps you'd care to elaborate?'

She shrugged. 'You've said many times that traditional family life isn't for you.'

'It isn't.'

'No. I realise that. But maybe there are some who don't quite believe you. You said yourself that people are guilty of believing what they want to believe. And what better way of discouraging any billionaire-hungry women intent on changing your mind than by parading your pregnant ex-lover and making it clear there is nothing between you? In one fell swoop you can demonstrate that your heir requirements have been satisfied, but your compartmentalised heart remains intact.'

There was silence for a moment before he spoke. 'Let me get this straight,' he said slowly, his silky voice edged with a frisson of danger. 'You're actually accusing me of using you as some sort of *prop* to help facilitate my reputation as a confirmed bachelor?'

Put like that, it *did* sound a bit harsh, but Lizzie's vexation was genuine. 'I don't know, do I? I don't know what you are or aren't capable of!' she howled. 'Because you never really talk to me, do you, Niccolò? Oh, you open your mouth and words come out—but I don't feel any closer to knowing you than when we spent that night together in the Cotswolds. And that's freaking me out. I don't want to give birth to the baby of a stranger. I want to be able to answer questions about you when our child asks. Because, believe me, he—or she—will ask about you one day.'

She paused long enough for him to enquire about the sex of their baby but—predictably—he didn't. 'I know that for a fact,' she added quietly, sucking in an unsteady breath, unable to stem her sudden stream of insecurity. 'When I was a little girl I was desperate to know more about my dad, but my mother was never able to tell me anything.'

'Why not?'

'Because after their one-night stand—yes, isn't it funny how history repeats itself?—she found out he was married and he said he would never leave his wife. She didn't even tell him she was having his baby and then, when she thought better of it...' Her words tailed off. 'I must have been about two months old at the time and I think she was depressed—she found out he'd been killed in a motorcycle accident. And that was the end of that,' she concluded bitterly. 'That's why I never knew my father and why I didn't want the same to happen to my own child.'

'Why didn't she—?'

'Why didn't she what?' Lizzie interrupted savagely. 'Go to his grieving young widow and inform her that her husband had been playing away? Lay herself open to rejection and censure—and for what? He was dead and he was never coming back.'

Niccolò nodded as he absorbed her words in silence, suddenly aware of what it must have taken for her to have tried so hard to find him, and now understanding why. He thought how unwittingly cruel he had been to her and wondered why she hadn't told him all this before.

Because you wouldn't have wanted her to. You always recoil when women try to tell you their life story, don't you?

'I'm sorry,' he said automatically.

But she shook her head, as if determined to

show him that she was not a victim. 'It's not your fault. It's not anybody's fault. But this…this situation is all wrong and the longer it goes on, the more confusing it will be, for everyone. It's time I went home.'

Niccolò found himself thinking how brave she'd been but now he saw the disquiet on her face, as if the emotion of it had all become too much. And even though on one level he knew he was bad news for her, he found himself unable to move, lost in a fog of feelings he didn't understand. It was hard to think straight and even harder to know the right thing to do. Well, that wasn't strictly true. His head told him exactly what he ought to do, but his body was telling him something entirely different. And Lizzie wasn't helping matters any. Her green eyes had grown smoky and he'd seen enough women look at him that way to know she wanted him. But she had to be sure. His lips twisted. Even if he wasn't.

'If you want to go back to England, I'm not going to stop you.'

'I wasn't expecting you to.'

'But that doesn't change the way I feel.'

'Oh?'

He saw the flare of hope in her eyes and forced himself to quash it, because this was nothing to do with romance and everything to do with desire. 'I want to carry on where we left off last night.'

The silence which followed this admission

seemed to stretch like a piece of elastic as the tension between them grew. He watched as her lashes lowered to conceal the flash of disappointment in her eyes, but when they fluttered open her gaze was dark and bold.

'So what's stopping you?' she asked quietly.

'How long have you got?' His laugh was short. 'Sense. Logic. Reason. The fact that nothing has changed. Not inside…' He slammed the flat of his hand against his chest, where his heart was. 'Here.'

Her pale green gaze clashed with his.

'I don't care,' Lizzie declared softly, because she didn't. It might be wrong—it was very definitely stupid—but there was only one thing she cared about right then and that was being in Niccolò's arms again. Because when he held her, he made her feel…*real*. And that was a very powerful feeling. She wanted him. She needed him— even if this was only ever going to be a bittersweet memory. Just do it, she thought, her desire spiked with hungry impatience.

But to her surprise he didn't. There was no demonstration of mind-blowing passion to make her instantly compliant and obliterate the remaining possibility of doubt. Instead his thumb traced a slow line down over her cheek and as he moved it away to examine it, she could see a small daub of silver paint on the whorled skin of his thumb-print.

'I was painting the little bell on Blanche's collar,' she babbled in an explanation he hadn't asked for and, surprisingly, he smiled.

'Let's go to bed,' he said softly, lacing her fingers in his.

CHAPTER NINE

IT FELT VERY grown-up and slightly scary to be led by Niccolò Macario through the echoing corridors of the vast suite. Any of the hotel staff could have seen them! But the place was silent and empty as they shut the door of his bedroom—and Lizzie got her first sight of a room which made her own look as if it would be better suited to a doll's house. Outside the snow was still falling—white and ethereal and swirling—while inside the solid antique furniture emphasised the fundamental masculinity of the room. Just as the man before her did. How supremely powerful he looked, in his custom-made suit, the pale silk of his shirt managing to make his hair appear even blacker than usual. Yet, for once, his hard edge of control seemed absent. She could tell he was trying hard to control his breathing, but the urgent glitter of his eyes was a dead giveaway, even to her.

'Come here,' he whispered, and Lizzie went straight into his waiting arms, lifting up her face as he drove his lips down on hers—and it wasn't until they were both out of breath that he drew away and looked down into her face, his eyes hot with hunger.

'Do you know how long I have been thinking about doing this to you?' he growled.

'How long?' she said breathlessly.

'Since I walked out of that door, back in the summer—there hasn't been a single day when I haven't fantasised about this.'

She was about to admit to the same such longings, but then he started kissing her again and the moment was lost.

She made an inadequate little gulp of protest as he picked her up and carried her over to the bed—the additional weight of her pregnancy not seeming to bother him at all. But his hands were gentler than Lizzie remembered as he began to remove her painting smock and the rest of her clothes, until she was left in nothing but her underwear. She should have been nervous, but nerves weren't getting a look-in, because wasn't there something incredibly flattering about the slight unsteadiness of his fingers as he whipped back the snowy counterpane and laid her down on his vast bed?

His hand reached behind to unfasten her new bra with its miracle underpinning and her breasts came tumbling out, bigger than he would have remembered them. For a moment he just stared at them, before bending his head to slowly kiss each peaking nipple, and Lizzie moaned beneath the lick of his tongue, turned on by the contrast of his tousled black head against her freckled skin. Next came her panties, slithered down over trembling thighs before he unceremoniously flicked those aside too. His black gaze raked over her with a burning intensity, but as it lingered briefly on the curve of her belly she saw his eyes cloud with something which looked like pain and instinctively, Lizzie shivered. Did he find the sight of her burgeoning body repulsive? Was he about to change his mind?

'Is something wrong?' she whispered.

But he shook his head, scooping up the discarded duvet and floating it down on top of her as if he couldn't wait to cover her up.

'You're cold,' he remarked matter-of-factly.

Lizzie thought about all the things she could say and knew one thing for sure. She might not get another chance to do this—so why waste it by playing games? She didn't feel cold. She felt strong and vital. She didn't want him swathing her in bubble wrap and treating her as if she were made of glass. She wanted him as man to her woman. As equals. Even if it were for one night only. Just like last time. 'I'm not,' she contradicted. 'Just excited.'

'Well, that's a coincidence because so am I.' He gave an unsteady laugh. 'And this has been a long time in the waiting.'

She watched as he began to undress, removing his clothes unselfconsciously, as if this was something he'd done many times before—which of course, he must have done. But Lizzie forced herself not to focus on the differences which existed between them. It didn't matter how many lovers he'd had before her. What mattered was being here now. With him. And he wasn't thinking of other women—not if that hungry expression on his face was anything to go by. He stepped out of the silken boxer shorts which had made no secret of his arousal, but seeing him completely naked drove home just how physically well endowed he was.

Did her face betray her flicker of apprehension? Was that why he came towards her, sitting on the edge of the bed while he stroked away the tumbled strands of her hair?

'Changing your mind is always a viable option, but sooner might be better than later,' he commented wryly.

As Lizzie shook her head, it occurred to her that he might actually *want* her to cancel this. Did he? Wouldn't that be more sensible for both of them, in the long run? Well, too bad. If that was really what he wanted then he was going to have to do the ejecting because she couldn't move. She didn't want to do anything except drink in all his strength and magnificence. 'That's not going to happen,' she whispered boldly, her hand trailing slowly over the rocky muscles of his arm.

'This is all new to me.' His words were urgent

as he got into bed and pulled her into his arms. 'I've never had sex with a pregnant woman before.'

'I should hope not.' But it thrilled her to think this was something he'd never done before. That she was his first, just as he had been for her. She shivered as he began to touch her, featherlight fingertips whispering over her skin. With rapt preoccupation, he stroked her breasts, her hips, her thighs…though she noticed he steered well clear of her belly. 'You won't hurt me,' she whispered. 'Intercourse is allowed. At least, that's what the clinic told me.'

He drew back from her, his black eyes narrowed. 'You were asking the clinic about sex?' he demanded.

Lizzie knew he had no right to be so proprietorial, but that didn't stop her from basking in the possessive husk of his tone. 'It's all part of their general advice,' she said. 'The staff go out of their way to make you realise that having sex during pregnancy is perfectly normal and nothing to be frightened of.'

She waited for him to ask more. To ask the question she'd been longing for him to ask ever since he'd turned up on that cold winter's day in London. But he didn't and she felt the sudden twist of her heart. He didn't *want* to know about the sex of their child and either she accepted that, or she shouldn't be here. He lowered his head and began to kiss her and she wasn't sure if he'd done it to silence her, or reduce her to a state where she wasn't thinking properly. But it worked. He kissed her until she was mindless with longing. Her nipples prickled and her tummy tightened—a rush of pure heat flooding her as his hand reached between her legs.

'Oh,' she said faintly, as his finger flicked out a delicate rhythm and she lay star-fished against his mattress.

'Oh, what?' he whispered.

'I don't remember,' she whispered back.

She knew she was probably being too passive but she couldn't seem to stop herself. She couldn't even think straight as waves of sensation began to swamp her and soon she was convulsing around his questing finger and choking out little moans of satisfaction.

His lips against her hair, he cradled her in his arms and for a while she just lay there in warm silence while her senses slowed and righted themselves. And didn't some fragment of her mind wonder whether he had deliberately bombarded her with pleasure while demanding none for himself because it gave him back all the control and left her with none?

'I want to be inside you,' he said roughly, as if he had read her thoughts, and Lizzie was taken aback by just how relieved she felt.

'I want that too,' she said, almost shyly—which was slightly ironic in the circumstances. She was heavy with his child, for heaven's sake—and yet she was behaving like a virgin. But what happened next wasn't what she had been hoping for. His lips and his fingers were as dextrous as ever, but there was something almost *mechanical* about his actions as he gently turned her onto her side and began to play with her nipples from his position behind her. It was a turn-on most definitely, but it wasn't in the least bit emotional.

Yet still she reacted. She couldn't help herself. She could feel his muscular body pressing against her back. The unmistakable nudge of his erection butting against her bottom. The powerful, hair-roughened thighs so hard against her soft flesh. A slug of desire hit her as his fingers reacquainted themselves with her moist folds and he began to strum her until she was mindless with longing once more.

'Do you like it like this, Lizzie?' he murmured into her ear, as his finger feathered up and down over her slick skin. 'Does it feel okay?'

She knew exactly what he meant. He was solicitously enquiring about her welfare—and hadn't the nurse at the clinic explained that this kind of position worked especially well for pregnant women? How the hell did he know *that*? Had he been reading books on the subject, or was it simply intuition? But it wasn't what she had been longing for. She wanted him to turn her over so she could look at him. She wanted to watch his face as he entered her, because that seemed like the ultimate intimacy which her foolish heart was craving. She wanted to get close to him, in ways which were more than just physical.

But he didn't.

It seemed that while she was silently praying for one thing, he seemed intent on doing the exact opposite. And God forgive her, but her body didn't seem to care. She was in total thrall to him, opening her thighs so that he could make that first thrust, and she shuddered with ecstasy. She could feel him. Hear him. She grabbed hold of his hand and began to suck on his thumb so she could taste him, too. But she couldn't see him. And because sight was the only one of her senses not engaged, she clamped her eyelids closed. But in a funny sort of way the lack of visual stimulation added an extra layer to her enjoyment, because it made everything seem so intense. And anonymous. Was that what he was aiming for?

Hot and hard, he increased his rhythm and Lizzie was so caught up as she was taken on that delicious ride with him that suddenly nothing else existed. Nothing but intense pleasure and the tumult of sensation. She heard him moan and suddenly she was moaning, too—her body clenching around him as he jerked out his seed.

She lay there, lost in a daze as he absently kissed her bare shoulder. She must have fallen asleep and so did he, because when next she became aware of her surroundings, she was lying tangled in his arms. His breathing was slow and steady—his lashes two black arcs set in golden olive skin and, once she had stopped drinking in his sheer gorgeousness, Lizzie realised this was her opportunity. Because if he couldn't open up to her at a moment like this, then when could he?

'So…' She touched her fingers to the dark curve of his jaw. 'Are you going to tell me something about yourself now, Niccolò Macario?'

Thick lashes fluttered open to reveal the obsidian gleam of his black eyes, but the expression on his mouth was hard. 'Is that the price I must pay for what just happened?'

'Is that how you think the world works?' She blinked. 'That everything has a price?'

'Because it does. We both know that,' he said silkily. 'Just like everything happens for a reason. Cause and effect. It's simple.'

'Does that mean you're not going to answer my questions?'

'I would prefer not to. But if you insist, I won't evade them. Unless,' he murmured, running a slow finger from her neck to her cleavage, 'you can think of something else we could do other than talking.'

It was a deliberate attempt to distract her and he *still* hadn't gone anywhere near her bump. Lizzie wriggled away from him fractionally, even though the drift of his finger felt wonderfully enticing. 'I'm asking on behalf of our child,' she said firmly, and then spoke the words she had been rehearsing in her head for so long. 'You do realise I don't know anything about you? Not even where you were born.'

Niccolò stared into her flushed features and gave a heavy sigh, recognising that the time for prevarication was over, no matter how much he wished it was otherwise. Because he owed her this. He knew that. But that didn't make it any easier to say things he'd kept buried for nearly two decades. Secrets he'd never divulged to anyone. Not even the therapist one of his enlightened college tutors had insisted he see, although the association hadn't lasted beyond a few uncomfortable, silent sessions. Because hadn't he always guarded his past as if it were a caged and dangerous beast? He'd locked it away in a dark and inaccessible place, which nobody could get at.

'I was born in Turin.'

'Rich boy? Poor boy?' she questioned succinctly, stretching out her legs so that her bare thigh brushed against his. 'A somewhere in between boy?'

'My father was one of Italy's most successful industrialists,' he clipped back. 'I grew up in one of the wealthiest suburbs of the city, with a summer home on the Amalfi coast, and was afforded every privilege a young boy could possibly want. Does that answer your question?'

'Some of them. I've got plenty of others. How about brothers and sisters?'

It was a natural question but his instinct was to deflect it. To provide the stock response he'd cultivated years ago, which would terminate the subject and make it clear that pursuing it would be crossing a forbidden line. But her thigh was still touching his and her silken hair was trailing over his arm and she felt little short of…amazing. As she lay there, her expression ridiculously trusting, Niccolò realised he had put himself in a honey trap of his own making. How could he possibly short-change the mother of his child when she was look-ing at him like that, even though the truth would change the way she looked at him for ever?

'For a long while it was just me,' he said slowly. 'My parents tried very hard to have another child. In fact, it dominated pretty much every facet of their lives—and mine. They'd almost given up hope, and then my…' How could his voice still falter like this, even after all these years? 'My sis-ter was born.'

'How old were you?'

'Fourteen.'

'That must have been…difficult.'

It was a perceptive remark but she spoke matter-of-factly, and in a way her lack of emotion was making it easy for him to continue. 'Yeah. Over-night, my life changed. My parents were com-pletely obsessed with Rosina but how could they not be, when...' His voice shook as pain ripped through his heart. 'When she was such a beautiful little girl.'

'You must have loved her very much,' she said, into the brittle silence which followed.

'I killed her.'

Her face blanched but she didn't leap from the bed and stare at him in horror and disbelief. Hadn't part of him hoped she might? So that the sweet look of trust would be wiped from her face, leaving him in peace to nurse his enduring guilt and his shame.

'Tell me,' she said simply.

That was all. A small, quiet query which somehow managed to pierce his heart, like a blade. Was that why it was so effective? So that suddenly the words were tumbling from his lips in a way which the highly paid therapist had never managed to achieve. The hand which had been resting in her hair clenched into a tight fist. 'Everything at home was about the baby,' he said hoarsely. 'And at school my classmates teased me relentlessly about the fact that my parents were still having sex.'

'And did you care?'

'I tried not to let it get to me.' He had cultivated a policy of not reacting. Of letting things bounce off him and showing the world he didn't give a toss. Until the day his insouciance had finally cracked. He remembered the temperature gauge creeping upwards. The slow whir of the air-conditioning. The creak of the old-fashioned lift.

'It was the summer holidays and it was unbearably hot in the city, but little Rosina didn't travel well, so we had been there for the entire school break.' He remembered feeling invisible. And bored. Nobody had been around. There had been nothing to do and no one to see. And then the invitation had landed on his mat—with all its bright and glimmering possibility.

'One of my schoolfriends invited me to his birthday party in the mountains. There would be people I hadn't seen all summer. Girls. One girl in particular. My parents refused to let me go.' It had seemed unjust to treat him like a child when he had been trying so hard to behave like a grown-up. He remembered the anger which had flared up inside him. 'So I sneaked out and hitchhiked there.' He paused. 'I lost my virginity that night and I lost track of time.'

'Oh,' she said, but he couldn't miss the crumpling of her face.

'My mother was going out of her mind with worry,' he continued, words firing from his mouth like bullets. 'My father was away on business and so she strapped Rosina in the car and set off up the mountains to come and get me. It was a clear night and visibility was good. There were no other cars around and my mother was a brilliant driver. But somehow...' His tone slowed. 'Somehow the car left the road and ended up in pieces on the ground, and by the time they found them, my mother and my sister were both...' The tightness in his chest was making it impossible for him to get the word out—but he had to. 'Dead.'

'Niccolò—'

'Don't,' he bit out. 'Don't say it.'

'You don't know what I was going to say.'

'Yes, I do. That it wasn't my fault. It was. If I hadn't gone to that party, it would never have happened. My mother and my sister wouldn't have died and my—'

She looked at him curiously as his words were severed. 'What?' she said softly. 'What?'

'Can't you see it doesn't matter, Lizzie?' he ground out bitterly. 'None of it matters. Not any more. It's done. Cause and effect, remember? End of story. I have to live with what I have done and it has informed my life ever since. It is why I am the man I am, and why I can never be the man for you. I am cold. I am cruel. So maybe you are right to go back to England and not spend a moment longer here than you need to. You need to find a man who can care for you. Who can love you in a way that I can never do. Who can protect you.'

'Niccolò—'

'No!' he negated furiously. 'I won't discuss it any more. There is no point.'

'Are you quite sure about that?'

He was taken off guard by the soft wash of understanding in her voice and even more by the way she rolled over to face him, so that her belly was touching his. That curved and alien shape he'd been trying so hard to avoid, even when he'd been making love to her. And then he felt it. Faint but unmistakable. Weak but immeasurably strong. The kick of a tiny limb. The tremble of new life. Their eyes met as an iron shackle was tightened around his heart and for a moment he couldn't speak. But what right did he have to this child, or any child?

'I'm very sure,' he said at last. 'I want to get my old life back. I never wanted to be a father. How many times do I have to tell you that, before you start believing me, Lizzie? I'll be doing you both a favour,' he added roughly.

'It doesn't feel that way right now.'

The hurt tone of her voice stabbed at his conscience and Niccolò could feel emotional chaos beckoning like an old enemy. She had been right to tell him she was leaving. Better to end this madness now and give them both some much-needed peace of mind. But somehow her arms had entwined themselves around his neck and she was clinging to him and—God help him—he was kissing her again and she was kissing him back. The sexiest, sweetest, yet most womanly kiss he could ever have imagined.

'Lizzie,' he said brokenly, against her lips.

'Shh…'

It seemed that his erstwhile virgin was now in

control and required no interruption. She drew her mouth away from his, as if to concentrate fully on his body, and he wondered afterwards if her hands were stroking over his flesh like that because she wanted to demonstrate her power over him, which at that moment was considerable. But then he stopped caring. He was lost in the responses she was inciting. Powerless to do anything other than comply with her sweet ministrations. Maybe it was his body's need to block out the bitterness of his thoughts which made his physical reaction to her so instant and overwhelming.

'Lizzie,' he gasped as her fingertips skated across his sternum—making a slow, sensual foray over each hard nipple. He held his breath as the flat of her hand reached the bony jut of his hip and she brushed her palm tantalisingly over the rigid throb of his erection and then away again. 'Please,' he said at last, when she did it again and again, and he thought he could bear no more.

Her fingers encircled him, sliding up and down the rigid shaft to create a light, soft rhythm. Her movements were dextrous and sure and he felt his eyes flutter to a close, helpless to resist the coming storm. And when he was almost there, she wriggled down the bed, her long hair brushing against his groin. Gently, she clamped her mouth around him, that soft imprisonment sending him under. He gripped onto her silken shoulders as he felt the powerful spurt of his seed into her mouth and when the last spasm had died away, he opened his eyes to see her licking her lips, like a satisfied pussycat.

It was possibly the most erotic but certainly the most intimate thing which had ever happened to him, and probably why he pushed back against it and felt the urgent need to escape. He shoved aside the rumpled bedclothes and got out of bed, seeing her look of bewilderment and, yes, hurt, but he shut his mind to it. He didn't want to be distracted by her nakedness, or her growing sexual confidence, or to have to dodge a stream of soft sympathy he had no right to. He didn't want to feel a child he had never asked for kicking against him like that. Or to see the woman he had impregnated boldly swallowing his seed. It was too much. He felt as if he'd lost a layer of his skin and she had been instrumental in that loss. As if Lizzie Bailey had somehow clawed it away from him, leaving him raw and exposed.

Turning his back on her, he picked up his discarded shirt and pulled it roughly over his shoulders, thinking he'd use one of the other bathrooms, rather than prolong this unbearable intimacy. He tugged on his trousers and by the time he turned back to her, he had recovered himself. But his brief flirtation with the past was over. She was right. It was the future she needed to negotiate. A future without him—and the sooner that happened, the better. Should he wait until she was dressed, until tempers and passions had cooled? And how long would that be? What if it was another day? A week. Prolonging this sweet torture of wanting her while knowing he needed to push her away, for both their sakes?

Steeling his heart against the crumpling of her lips, he slanted her a gritty smile. 'We need to think about income.'

'*Income?*' she echoed.

'Don't look so horrified, Lizzie. I assume you're not going to turn down a reasonable settlement just because we're not together? I don't imagine you're going to make enough from your dog portraits to live on.'

'Don't you *dare* trash my work!'

'I'm not. I happen to think your work is great.' His voice gentled and he wished she wouldn't look at him that way. He wished she weren't flushed and vulnerable beneath the rumpled duvet. He wished for a lot of things, but they were never going to happen. His throat tightened. 'I'm just being practical, that's all.'

'Yes, I know you are,' she said, a note of bitterness entering her voice. 'Practicality is something you're good at, isn't it, Niccolò?'

'You're making it sound like a character flaw.'

'Because sometimes I think it is!' she snapped back.

'I will buy you somewhere to live—be assured of that,' he continued coolly. 'A house, or an apartment. Big or small. Whatever you like. It's yours. Just let my office know.'

'Yeah. Thanks.'

But her words sounded automatic. As if she was saying them because she had no choice, rather than acting like a woman who had just hit the jackpot. But the way she *felt* about his offer was nothing to do with him, he reminded himself grimly. He just needed to get his old life back. The welcome solitude of domestic isolation and the complete absence of emotional disruption. 'Oh, I nearly forgot.' He walked across the room to the jacket he'd slung on a chair and fished something out of the pocket. 'Lois asked me to give you this.'

She surveyed the frayed piece of fabric in his hand. 'What is it?'

'It's Blanche's favourite blanket,' he explained. 'Apparently, the dog originally belonged to Lois's neighbour, and she knitted it. And when the old lady died…' He shrugged and, infuriatingly, his voice had a slight crack to it. 'Lois took the animal in.'

This story, told to him by his obviously emotional assistant, had been yet another thing he hadn't needed to hear, and he blamed Lizzie for that, too. He didn't *want* that kind of interaction with members of his staff. He wanted his world to go back to normal. A world where Lois organised his meetings and fielded phone calls, not where she started fumbling for a crumpled-up tissue, her eyes filling with tears while she told him some sob-story about a dog. A world where he could start dating other women again who wouldn't niggle and get underneath his skin.

'You said you wanted something particular belonging to the animal to enhance your portrait, and this is it,' he finished on a growl as he dropped the ragged piece of fabric on the bed. 'I'll ask my office to arrange your flight back to England.'

She nodded, like a reluctant father of the bride, forced to make an unwanted speech at a wedding. 'You know, despite everything you've said, you can always change your mind, Niccolò.'

'About us?'

'No, not about us. Don't worry—I'm getting that particular message loud and clear. About the baby. I will make it as easy as I can for you, if you decide that fatherhood is something you want to embrace. Even if...' She swallowed and assumed a bright smile. 'No matter who you bring with you,' she amended quickly. 'You will always be welcome in our child's life.'

Niccolò winced because, in a way, her quiet dignity made him feel even worse, if that were possible. But he wasn't going to promise something he could never deliver, so he just nodded his head.

'Oh, and I've left the drawing I did of you in your office.'

His eyes narrowed. She hadn't mentioned it again and he'd assumed she'd forgotten all about it. 'But I didn't give you any photographs to work from,' he objected.

'I know you didn't. I did it from…well, for once I did it from memory. I've wrapped it up in brown paper because I didn't think you'd want the staff gawping at it.'

Silently, he nodded, forcing himself to tear his eyes away from the rumpled bedclothes, which bore all the hallmarks of their incredible love-making, and then to retreat from his own room, as if Lizzie Bailey's pale green gaze and freckled proximity had the power to contaminate him. The power to make him feel stuff he just wanted to forget.

CHAPTER TEN

LIZZIE STARED OUT of the bus window, lost in thought as she waited for the stubborn sheep to stop blocking the mud-splattered country lane. It was strange really. She hugged her arms across her chest as raindrops trickled down the windows. When you were broke—particularly if you were going through a slightly dodgy time—you thought that having loads of money would be the silver bullet to solve all your problems.

She sighed.

How wrong could she have been?

Because it didn't feel like that at all.

She was no longer *poor* Lizzie, scrimping and saving with the ever-constant worry that her boss might not be able to cope with the sound of a crying baby and throw her out on the streets. She had been back in England for nearly a month and it seemed she was now rich Lizzie. Her bank manager had called to request a private meeting and she had been summoned into his office and offered a cup of tea *and* a biscuit, while the man had talked to her in almost reverential tones about her new 'portfolio'.

And that was the power of money, she guessed. After a lifetime of terse communications about the state of her overdraft and wondering if she should cut up her credit card, she was now flavour of the month. Because while she'd been on the flight back from America, Niccolò Macario had deposited a vast sum of money into her account, his brief email informing her that if there were insufficient funds for her needs, she should speak to his office and ask for more.

Insufficient funds? Was he insane? Maybe if she was planning on putting in an offer on Windsor Castle, or if she fancied acquiring a fleet of expensive racehorses, then she might feel a tad stretched. But despite the ridiculous amount he had given her, Lizzie had been bitterly disappointed by the way he'd gone about it. It had all been so cold-blooded and compartmentalised. So hands-off and distant.

The stubborn sheep trundled into a nearby field and the bus began to move again. What had she expected? It seemed a bit churlish to rail against the billionaire's generosity, but it did feel as if he was paying her off. As if he was throwing a lot of money at her to keep her quiet.

But that was the kind of man he was.

He had told her there was no future for them, just before she'd made that ill-advised trip to his bedroom, and no amount of wishing otherwise was going to change that simple fact. Had she imagined that the amazing sex which had followed would be enough to change his mind? That he might miss her as much as she missed him? Because she did. She missed him with a pain which was almost physical.

She closed her eyes.

But he didn't want to be involved in her life in any way. That was the whole point of giving her a lump sum. She was free to do as she pleased. Free as a bird. Free from any involvement with the father of her child. And if that state of affairs wasn't to her liking, well, she would have to get used to it and, eventually, move on. She bit her lip, praying it happened sooner rather than later, because surely this constant aching in her heart was unsustainable.

Yet even though it was pointless, sometimes at night she couldn't stop herself remembering *his* pain. The unbearable bleakness on his face when he'd told her about the deaths of his mother and baby sister. The terrible weight of shame and guilt which had surrounded him had been almost palpable and she'd thought how alone he had seemed in that moment. Her heart had gone out to him, but the grim and unremitting expression on his face had warned her that he would not welcome her sympathy. But it had become instantly understandable why his behaviour had been so contradictory. Why he didn't want a family of his own, because he had experienced the indescribable anguish of a child's death.

Lizzie swallowed. Was that why he had been so protective of her? She remembered his face in the park when he had found her—raw and ravaged with pain, his words whipping through the icy air.

I thought I'd lost you.

And where had his father been during all the heartbreak he had suffered? He hadn't mentioned that. Not once. There were so many questions she hadn't asked him and would now never get the chance. So let it go, she told herself, as her hand rested on the curve of her baby bump. She wasn't doing herself or little Freddy any favours, lying awake obsessing about a man who didn't want her. A man who had suggested she go out and find someone else!

With no ties and a reasonable budget, she could afford to live pretty much anywhere she wanted, but the anonymity of a big city left her cold. Despite the bittersweet memories it invoked, she found herself drawn back to the Cotswolds, where she'd worked for longest as a housekeeper and which still felt like the closest thing she'd ever had to home. With no desire to move this side of Christmas, she started renting a cottage, joined a prenatal exercise class and met other mums-to-be. And even though she was the only person in the class without a partner, Lizzie convinced herself it didn't matter. Her mood brightened considerably when the teacher asked if she could possibly paint a portrait of her mother's Maine Coon and Lizzie cautiously agreed. She had never attempted painting a cat before, but she certainly wasn't going to turn down a commission.

On Christmas Eve, she did what she had been wanting to do ever since she'd got back, even though it went against her better judgement. She drove past Ermecott Manor, expecting to see a giant Christmas tree blazing outside the Jacobean mansion, but to her surprise, the house was in darkness. Perhaps the family who'd bought it had gone back to Scotland for the holidays. For a minute she just sat in the car staring at it, but then she started up the engine and set off again. Why was she choosing the most emotional night of the year to remind herself that this was where it had all started?

It was almost dusk by the time she arrived back at the cottage and Lizzie had just switched on a string of fairy lights and lit the fire, when she heard a knock on the door. She froze, her heart beginning to race like a train as she was filled with the senseless hope it might be Niccolò. But it wasn't. It was a driver from a local delivery company, struggling beneath the shape of a huge and cumbersome-looking package, which she hauled from the back of the van.

'Let me carry it in for you,' the woman said, after a cursory glance at Lizzie's extended belly.

'That's very kind of you. There isn't a lot of room, but over here would be lovely.'

After the woman had left, Lizzie unpacked the package with curious fingers, peeling back the cardboard wrapping to find an easel inside. For a moment, she just sat there and stared at it. It was handmade and very beautiful. The kind of thing she had always dreamed of owning. Running her hand over the smooth beech wood, she searched for the sender's name—though she knew there was only one person who would have sent something like this. And yes. There it was.

She picked up the note.

Hopefully you'll get a chance to use this before and after the baby is born. Niccolò

It was brief and typewritten, and for a moment she wondered if it was some kind of olive branch, until she forced herself to see sense. It had probably been suggested by Lois, and dictated by her. She mustn't start reading things into a simple message. When they'd parted in Manhattan they had agreed to be civil and courteous, and this was obviously a demonstration that he intended to keep his word. It was a very kind gesture and she would send him an equally brief and polite thank you note in return.

But Lizzie couldn't resist picking up the phone and telephoning him in America, her fingers trembling as the call connected too quickly to allow for a change of mind.

'Niccolò?'

'Lizzie.'

It was only weeks since she'd heard his voice but it seemed like a whole lifetime as his rich accent rippled over her skin like velvet. She closed her eyes. 'Thank you for the easel.'

'Do you like it?'

'It's...beautiful.' She hesitated as she studied her reflection in the mirror—the fecund woman who stared back—and imagined Niccolò in his sleek penthouse, with all the sleek people who comprised his friendship circle. 'I haven't bought you anything.'

'I wasn't expecting you to.'

'Because you're the man who has everything?'

There was a pause. 'So they say.'

She drew in a breath, the pleasure of talking to him again almost cancelled out by the pain. Because that's the reality, she thought bitterly. He might not have everything he needs, but he certainly has everything he wants.

'Anyway, there's the pencil drawing you did of me,' he continued.

'What did you think of it?'

'It was...interesting,' he concluded, without elaboration.

Wasn't interesting one of those polite words people used when they didn't like something?

The silence stretched, and Lizzie thought about all the things they weren't saying. The conversation which was going on in her head, which was so different from the one which was actually happening. She wanted to ask why he'd sent her this Christmas present out of the blue and whether he recognised that it ran the risk of sending out the wrong sort of signals to a woman who was missing him so much. She wanted to ask if he missed her, and if he'd slept with anyone else since she'd been back. But she said none of these things, just wished him happy holidays, and then hung up.

But she dreamt about him that night and the dreams were uncomfortably vivid and Lizzie decided that a half-life of communication was only going to hold her back. He could make contact about the baby whenever it suited him, but she was never going to ring him again, not even if he sent her a diamond necklace.

On Christmas Day she pulled crackers, ate turkey and manufactured having the best time with the kind couple from the antenatal group who had invited her to share their lunch. And in the quiet days which followed, she worked hard on her painting of Fluffy, the Maine Coon—why *were* people so unoriginal when it came to naming their pets? she wondered.

Having an easel in the cottage was a real game-changer—even if it was always going to be associated with Niccolò. But at least painting had always been a distraction and never had she needed it quite as much as she did at the moment. Her brush dabbed rapidly against the canvas and Lizzie was so engrossed in getting Fluffy's eyes just right that initially she mistook the knock for the branches of the climbing rose being battered against the door by the howl of the winter wind. But when the knock was repeated, some second sense made her grow still and a trickle of excitement whisper down her back. Don't be so stupid, she thought as she opened the cottage door. Why would it be Niccolò?

But it *was* him. All dark virile power, his thick hair ruffled by the wind, the breadth of his shoulders emphasised by the dark cashmere coat he was wearing. Against the frosty, dusky day, he looked amazing—black eyes glittering like polished jet, in the sheen of golden olive skin. The impact of seeing him was so visceral that her breath dried in her throat, but she recognised that the powerful pull he exerted was more than simply sexual attraction.

Because this was the father of her baby. A bond had been forged between them which could never be broken. He had let her walk out of his life and told her he didn't want to be part of hers. But he was here, wasn't he? Lizzie's heart was filled with a rush of hope but she tried not to let it show, because it was tempered by fear. And wasn't her biggest fear that he might hurt her all over again, and she would just keep coming back for more?

So don't lay yourself open to it, she told herself. Protect yourself from this cold, sexy man who finds it easy to make expansive gestures. He can buy you houses and confuse the hell out of you by sending unexpected presents, but he doesn't want love.

And while it was all very well agreeing to be polite to one another—wasn't he bending the rules by turning up here without warning?

'Niccolò!' she exclaimed. 'Why didn't you tell me you were coming?'

Niccolò's eyes met hers and saw the unmistakable flicker of challenge flickering from their pale green depths. 'Perhaps I thought you might refuse to see me,' he said slowly.

'That would be extremely foolish, since you're the one who's financing my life,' she said flippantly. 'Don't they say you should never bite the hand that feeds you? I'm guessing that the easel was a sweetener?'

Niccolò flinched as her accusatory words washed over him. Was that how she saw him now—as her provider, but nothing else? And could he blame her if she did? 'I wonder, is this a conversation we should be having on the doorstep?'

'Well, there's nobody around to hear us so I'm not worried about that, but it *is* a cold day.' She shrugged. 'So I guess you'd better come in.'

She opened the door wider and he stepped inside and closed the door, though he noticed how quickly she moved away from him, as if any kind of contact was something to be avoided at all costs. Bending his head to avoid the low beams on the ceiling, he went to stand by the fire.

'If you sit down, I'll make you a cup of tea,' she said.

Niccolò gave a reluctant nod. He didn't want to sit down, and he didn't particularly want a cup of tea, for the English national beverage had never really appealed to him. In truth, all he wanted was to feast his eyes on her, but in her current spiky mood it might be best to humour her. He looked around, assessing the place Lizzie Bailey had chosen to make her home, taken aback by its modesty, though Lois—for the two women had continued to communicate—had informed him that Lizzie was renting something 'quirky'.

His eyes narrowed. She certainly hadn't decided to flash the cash he had given her, that was for sure. The cottage was homely, but small—though the room was alive with colour and warmth from the fire. Flickering light from the flames danced on the bare walls, splashing shades of coral and gold over the half-painted canvas of a rather terrifying-looking cat, which stood on the easel.

He could hear her crashing around in the kitchen, the noisy demonstration of domesticity worlds away from the carefully orchestrated mealtimes which had resumed in his hotel suite in Manhattan, and the irony of that didn't escape him. Because hadn't he discovered that the peace and quiet he had craved could suddenly feel like a vacuum? All the things he'd thought he was missing weren't everything they were cracked up to be, something which was being hammered home to him every second of every day. His lips twisted. Be careful what you wished for.

A few moments later she emerged from the kitchen carrying a loaded tray and he walked over to her.

'Here. Let me.'

'It's quite all right,' she said firmly. 'I'm perfectly capable of doing it myself. I'm not some clinging vine, Niccolò. How do you think I manage when you're not here? I don't need a man to lean on.'

Despite her spirited objections, Niccolò overrode her protests and took the tray from her, putting it down on the table. But neither of them sat. They just surveyed each other from opposite ends of the weathered surface—as if they were about to engage in a duel. Her expression was mulish as she stared at him, but this was the perfect vantage point from which to study her. She was wearing a paint-spattered smock, with a scarf wrapped round her head, so that stray strands of pale red hair were escaping from their confinement. Her cheeks were rounder since he'd last seen her and so was her belly. Had the removal of complications in her life—like him—contributed to her glowing appearance? Pregnancy suited her, he realised with a sudden ache as he thought how long it had been since he'd seen her in the flesh.

And it was nobody's fault but his own.

He had wanted Lizzie Bailey out of his life, never dreaming her absence could leave such a hole in his existence.

She pushed a plate towards him. 'Mince pies. Home-made.'

'I haven't come here to eat cake,' he growled.

'Well, they're not strictly cake, of course. These ones are made from orange pastry, filled with a spicy mixture of raisins and currants. I don't know if you're familiar with them in America but we...' And then she lifted the palms of her hands into the air before letting them fall helplessly to her sides. 'What am I *doing*? You turn up on my doorstep without so much as a phone call, and I start talking inanely about mince pies. What the hell is going on, Niccolò?'

He glanced at his watch. 'Before I answer your question, I'd like to take you for a drive.'

She narrowed her eyes suspiciously. 'Where?'

'If I told you, it would spoil the surprise.'

'But we are not a couple, Niccolò. And therefore, you shouldn't arrive on my doorstep like this, dangling surprises. It's not appropriate behaviour.'

'We haven't exactly been a model of appropriate behaviour from the get-go, have we?' he questioned drily. 'Please. Just come for a drive with me, Lizzie. Let's talk on neutral territory.'

'I didn't think there was anything left to say.' She stared at him defiantly but must have read the determination in his eyes, because she puffed out a sigh. 'Oh, very well. But I don't want to be long.'

He waited while she unwound the scarf from her hair, put a guard around the fire and slithered into the coat she'd bought in New York. But he had to subdue his fierce desire to button it up for her—recognising from the warning glint in her eyes that any such gesture would be unwelcome.

Outside, the wind was strong and icy as he led her towards the car.

'So. Where's the chauffeur today?' she questioned as he opened the passenger door for her.

'There is no chauffeur. I'm driving.'

'And are you any good?'

'What do you think, Lizzie?' he challenged softly and the way she bit her lip did something strange to his heart.

As he started the engine, neither of them spoke—but as they drove through the muddy lanes, he heard her give a sharp intake of breath and she turned to him.

'We're on the way to Ermecott Manor!'

He kept his eyes on the road ahead. 'Yep.'

'Why?'

'Why don't you wait and see?'

'I'm not sure I want to,' she moaned. 'I was up

there the other day. They were away for Christmas but they're probably back by now, and I don't want to be spotted lurking around the place like the Ghost of Christmas Past.'

But as the car swished down the driveway, the ancient house was still in darkness, the pale winter light of dusk surrounding it like a halo. Niccolò stopped the vehicle and went round to open the passenger door, and she got out and stared up at the impressive old house.

'Why have you brought me here?' she whispered, the sting of emotion in her voice.

'Because I've bought it.'

'*Bought* it? What are you talking about?' She shook her head. 'It isn't for sale. Sylvie sold it to a family from Scotland. They own it.'

'Not any more they don't.' There was a pause. 'I made them an offer they couldn't refuse.'

'Are you for real, Niccolò?' she demanded. 'People don't say things like that outside gangster films.'

'But it's true,' he said unapologetically. 'So why don't you come inside?'

Lizzie hesitated, filled with confusion, unsure why Niccolò had purchased the ancient property, yet overwhelmed by a very human desire to revisit a house which had meant so much to her. She could see it first, and then ask him. 'Okay,' she agreed grudgingly. 'Why not?

Once inside, he pressed a master light switch

and an instant glow illuminated the historic interior with a soft, apricot light. Lizzie scanned the immediate vicinity, reacquainting herself with all the nooks and crannies she knew so well. The bare bones of the beautiful structure remained intact. The carvings and moulded ceilings were just as she remembered them, as were the tiled floors and panelled hallways. But that air of faint neglect still existed and, of course, it was completely empty.

And there was that stupid broom cupboard down the hallway. A lump constricted her throat as memories of that sultry afternoon came flooding back. The feel of his fingers on her flesh and the taste of his lips. She could barely relate to the woman she had been then, who would behave so impetuously with a man she had only just met. Lizzie could feel herself flushing but now wasn't the time to be thinking about sex, or to remember how joyous and carefree everything had seemed on that golden afternoon when their child had been conceived. This was a different time, she told herself fiercely. And they were both in a different place.

Yet nothing had really changed in her feelings towards the man who had joined her in that crazy dance of passion, had it? She still felt the same potent pull of attraction—only now she knew him better, which complicated things even more. She actually *liked* him, even though she had tried very hard not to.

She turned to him, to find him studying her intently. 'Tell me why you've bought it,' she said.

'Because you love it. I remember you telling me so, that night we spent together here.'

Her hand crept up to her neck, as if to hide the pulse which was flaring so rapidly there. 'And what does that have to do with anything?' she questioned huskily.

He shrugged. 'I thought you might want to live here. Bring the baby up here. You'd have a generous budget to do up the place as you saw fit. I sensed how much you've always wanted to restore it, only you didn't have the necessary funds before.'

It was a gross distortion of her secret dreams but, no matter how painful it might prove to be, Lizzie knew she had to pick it apart. 'Just the two of us?' she verified. 'Me, and the baby?'

'Well, yes.' There was a pause. 'Unless you were prepared to consider an alternative scenario.'

'Go on.'

'I miss you, Lizzie,' he said. 'The apartment has felt empty without you, and I don't want you out of my life.'

'I see,' she said slowly, but she didn't, not really. Because they were weasel words. A double negative, or something like that. He wasn't actually saying he wanted her *in* his life, was he? Just that he didn't want her out of it.

His mouth hardened as if he was disappointed

by her understated response, and from his eyes glittered a strange, black light. 'We could even get married, if that's what you wanted,' he added harshly.

CHAPTER ELEVEN

As LIZZIE FROZE with what looked like genuine horror, Niccolò found himself thinking it wasn't a
particularly complimentary way to respond to a
proposal he had spent his life vowing he was never
going to make.

'Run that one past me again,' she said tightly.

'My lawyers think it would be a good idea. To
get married.'

'Your lawyers think it would be a good idea to
get married?'

'Is it really necessary to keep repeating everything I say?'

'I think it is. Just to check I haven't slipped into
some parallel universe. Because this is surreal,
Niccolò. In fact, it's beyond surreal.'

'But why?' he demanded. 'Isn't this what people
used to do in the old days? They honoured their
responsibilities, as I am prepared to honour mine.
As my wife, you will be afforded status, income
and security.' He paused. 'And, of course, inheri-

tance would be a much tidier issue for this baby, if he or she is my legal heir.'

Niccolò waited for the inevitable rush into his arms, the tears mingled with shouts of laughter as she accepted his proposal. But the face she presented to him was not the one he had expected to see. It was a militant face. Her eyes were flashing green fire and her colour had become heightened so that two bright spots burned at the centre of her cheeks.

'*This* baby? Is that all you can say? All you can *ever* say!' she declared, flicking back a lock of pale red hair with an angry hand. 'When are you going to start thinking about *this baby* as a person, Niccolò, rather than a thing—or is that too big a stretch?'

He flinched. 'That isn't fair.'

'Isn't it? Think about it. Not once—not *once*—have you asked me whether it's a boy or a girl.'

His voice was quiet. 'Do you know?'

Her voice was equally quiet. 'Yes, I know.'

His body tensed. 'Tell me.' His eyes met hers. 'Please.'

'It's a son,' she said, at last, her jaw working. 'You're having a son, Niccolò.'

Niccolò felt his heart clench. 'A boy,' he said hoarsely.

'A boy,' she agreed, her eyes scanning his face as if searching for clues. 'I call him Freddy.'

'Freddy,' he echoed as an unexpectedly powerful rush of emotion flooded through him and Niccolò couldn't work out whether it was relief, or sorrow. Or both. He knew he owed her some reaction to what she had just told him, but he couldn't give one. He felt weighted to the place where he stood, as if he were made of marble instead of flesh. As if this were happening to someone else, not him.

'I guess you must feel as if you've hit the jackpot,' she continued quietly.

He stared at her uncomprehendingly. 'What are you talking about?'

She shrugged. 'Isn't marriage just a way of securing your legal heir? Of getting what you want.'

'You think this is all about *me*?' He shook his head, hurt and angered by her assumption. 'I just want to do my best for you and the child. I am prepared to have you inherit the majority of my estate on any terms you like, and marriage makes that a whole lot easier. You must believe that, Lizzie.'

But she shook her head as she walked away from him, as if she needed a safe distance from which to glare at him.

'Money, money, money, that's all you seem to care about,' she declared, beginning to pace up and down the ornate reception room. 'You're going to be a father—yet not once have you mentioned your own father. Why not?'

Niccolò swallowed, the heavy weight of pain turning his heart into a lump of stone. 'You know more about me than anyone else. Yet still you want more. Because this is what women do,' he said bitterly. 'They grasp and grasp and are never satisfied. Well, you've had as much from me as I'm prepared to give, Lizzie. This is the man I am. You've heard what my offer is. Take it or leave it. So...' He raised his brows. 'What's it to be?'

A long silence followed as he waited for her inevitable capitulation, knowing he mustn't appear smug or triumphant.

'Actually... I'll leave it.' She sucked in an unsteady breath and stared at him. 'I don't want to bring my child...our child...up in that kind of way. In a cold, empty marriage where certain subjects are off-limits just because you say so.'

He stared at her, at first in disbelief and then with suspicion. 'If this is your way of trying to negotiate, Lizzie, I can tell you now that it won't work.'

'It isn't,' she said simply. 'It's the way I feel. The answer is no.'

'Then there's nothing more to be said, is there?' he questioned, his voice cooling. 'If you wait while I turn off the lights and close up the house, I'll drop you back at your cottage.'

Lizzie felt numb yet emotional as she got back into Niccolò's car, trying to process the things which had been said. She had to bite down very hard on her lip to stop it from trembling—glad the darkness hid the rapid blinking of her eyes as she attempted to keep rogue tears at bay. But her heart was twisted with pain and hurt and disappointment. She felt as if they'd come so close. He'd bought the house of her dreams, which was a pretty thoughtful thing to do. And though his marriage proposal hadn't been the stuff of fantasy, it had been a start—a foundation to work on. If he'd taken just one more step… If he'd opened up a little and let her get closer… But he hadn't. When it had come to the crunch, he had retreated from her questions and turned back into an emotional iceberg, and she couldn't live like that. It wasn't fair. Not to any of them.

Neither of them spoke during the journey back through the cold winter's night. She guessed there was nothing left to say. But when they reached the cottage, he insisted on opening the car door for her and seeing her safely up the path and Lizzie wanted to cry out—to *implore* him not to be so damned protective, because it was making her long for more of the same. But she was quickly brought back down to earth by his reluctance to set foot inside—as if the interior of her humble abode might contaminate him. She waited for him to mention Freddy, but he didn't do that either—and a fierce pride began to take shape inside her because she certainly wasn't going to *beg* him to talk about his unborn son. She suddenly pictured a future. A horribly realistic future, where the billionaire's occasional visits to see his unplanned offspring became more and more sporadic—until in the end they tapered off completely. She shivered.

'It's cold. Go inside,' he said roughly. 'And think about what you want to do. You can move in to Ermecott any time you like, but if you'd rather choose somewhere else to live, I will understand. Just let me, or my office, know.'

'I will.'

'Goodbye, Lizzie.'

'Goodbye.'

Niccolò turned away from her, steeling his heart against the sombre note in her voice, telling himself throughout the drive back to London that he had made the right decision—for all of them. He shook his head. She was ungrateful. Unrealistic. He couldn't give her what she wanted—and she wanted way too much.

He gave his car keys to the waiting valet. He would spend the night here at the hotel and have his plane made ready for his return flight to Manhattan in the morning. He would order dinner to be delivered to his suite and catch up on a little work, just as he always did.

But his gourmet meal remained untouched, and the figures on his computer screen were a meaningless blur. Night-time brought no relief either, for the hours were disturbed by images he couldn't seem to ignore. Of hair the colour of a faded Halloween pumpkin, and the softest lips he had ever kissed. Her sweet, virginal tightness. Her understanding. Angrily, he slammed his fist into the goose-down pillow, then turned to stare up at the ceiling as the pale glow of dawn crept in through the windows.

Better get used to it, he thought grimly, because this was his new normal.

He was free.

Unencumbered.

And he didn't like it.

He didn't like it one bit.

At breakfast time, the strongest coffee the Granchester hotel could offer didn't help, and his plate of eggs remained untouched. Several times he took out his phone to call his pilot, and several times he slid it back into his pocket. At a quarter after ten, he gave up the fight and retraced the drive he'd made last night, his mouth dry and his heart thumping as he stopped the car outside Lizzie's little cottage. He thumped on the door with his fist and when she answered, she didn't smile. She looked at him questioningly.

'I'd like to come in.'

'Sure. But I'm not sure we've got anything left to say to each other, Niccolò—particularly at the moment,' she responded calmly. 'So shall we just try and keep it amicable?'

His mouth grew even drier as he closed the door behind him and the pounding of his heart was almost deafening. The fire was unlit and the room was chilly and suddenly he knew there was no time for prevarication. 'You want to know why I've never talked about my father?' he demanded hoarsely. 'Because I don't know anything about him. Not any more. We haven't spoken for nearly twenty years,' he continued, dragging in a ragged breath, which burned his throat even more.

She had grown very still as she stood in front of him, her green eyes still burning with questions. Close enough for him to touch, but never had she seemed so distant.

'Not since the morning after the accident, when he told me that if I hadn't been so selfish then my mother and my sister would still be alive. That his child—his *favourite* child—wouldn't be lying in a satin-lined casket, surrounded by white roses.' His bitter laugh was edged with self-contempt. 'And that he wished above all else I could take her place.'

He could see her swallowing, her neck working convulsively as she tried to work out what to say, and suddenly all that distance was gone as her face grew soft. 'People often say things they don't mean in the heat of the moment, Niccolò.'

'But he *did* mean it. Every word,' he emphasised harshly. 'And since I wished for exactly the same fate, I accepted those words and his anger as my due. And that was the last time we spoke. He sent me away, to the home of my maternal grandmother.'

She seemed to absorb this. 'And what was that like?'

Now it was harder to speak. Harder to articulate words without his voice breaking. 'She lived in Tuscany. So you could say it was the perfect opportunity to discover one of the most beautiful regions of Italy.'

'What was it *like*, Niccolò?' she persisted quietly.

The pain of remembering twisted at his heart. Was that the reason why he had refused to think about it all these years? 'My grandmother adored her daughter and her granddaughter,' he said slowly. 'And she was obviously influenced by my father's version of the accident.' He swallowed. 'Like him, she held me responsible for their deaths and perhaps that was understandable.'

'And was she…cruel?'

'No, no. She fed me and provided a roof over my head and made sure I never missed school.' He paused. 'But she found it difficult to talk to me, without…censure, which was why I left Italy just as soon as I could and have never returned.'

Her green eyes had grown narrow. 'And did your father never try to reconcile with you?'

'Never. But in many ways, I was relieved. Too much water had flowed under that particular bridge and sometimes there is no way back from something like that.' He shook his head. 'You think I wanted to put myself—and him—through all that pain again?'

Lizzie bit her lip as his words died away and

the expression on his face was almost too much to bear. But she *had* to bear it. To share it. If they were to have any chance together, she couldn't let him suffer alone any more. And why else had he turned up this morning, if he wasn't still holding out for some kind of future for them? But, oh, hell. It was worse than she could ever have imagined. No wonder he had such problems with trust and relating to women, if his grandmother had subjected him to such a cold and silent punishment.

He had told her early on that love didn't feature in his vocabulary and now she could understand why. He was convinced he didn't know *how* to love, she realised, because nobody had ever shown him. His formative years had shaped him. A boy neglected by his parents as they sought to increase the size of their family. A father who could not live with the consequences of how that had impacted on their son's behaviour. And a grandmother who had been unable to see beyond her own grief to help the teenager who had been hurting so badly. No wonder Niccolò had become the man he had. No wonder he had pushed emotion away.

But surely he was underestimating himself. He might not be comfortable using the words, but at times he had *behaved* like a man who knew the true meaning of love. The question was—would he allow himself to believe it? Could she show him?

She *had* to show him. She had grown up without a father and many times had felt the absence of his presence. Why subject their baby to the same fate, if there was a chance it could be different?

But she wasn't just thinking as a mother, she realised. She was thinking as a woman, too. She wanted this man so much. This clever and complicated man who made her feel things she hadn't thought possible. Was there any way he could ever open up his heart and let her inside?

'I think your grandmother and your father were both hurting very badly,' she said slowly. 'And because of that, they lashed out at you and behaved in a way they shouldn't have done, and which made it much worse. But that's…' She drew in an unsteady breath. 'That's all in the past, Niccolò. It's the future we've got to think about now. So I'm going to start by saying that I really do appreciate you buying Ermecott for me.'

She hesitated as she met the granite of his features and she wondered if she'd imagined the faint flicker of relief in his eyes—as if she'd granted him a reprieve by sticking to practicalities. 'But don't you understand that, without you, it's just bricks and mortar?' she continued softly. 'It might as well be a shoebox on the side of the motorway, for all the appeal it would have. It would only be having you there with us which would make it into a real home.'

He gave a swift shake of his head. 'But I can't give you what you want. What you deserve. I can't give you love, Lizzie.'

'Are you quite sure about that?' she asked him. 'You see, I think you already have. You didn't want a baby—you were so, so clear about that. But despite all those reservations, you came to find me when you found out I was pregnant, and you scooped me up and gave me a place to stay, didn't you? You guarded and protected me in New York, and even though at times I thought it was a bit over the top, secretly, I absolutely loved it.

'Remember that day you rushed to find me in the snow? When you...' Her voice wobbled a little. 'When you took off your own coat and put it on my back and buttoned it up, and it felt like the most caring thing anyone had ever done for me. Well, actually—it was. You've supported me and continue to support me. You've tried to do your best by me and the baby, but you haven't told me any lies along the way. You might not think you're capable of love, Niccolò Macario, but I do. Love is not what you say, but what you do, and I'm prepared to hang around long enough for you to recognise that.'

She swallowed. 'And just in case you should be in any doubt of my feelings for you, I'm putting it on the record that I love you. I love you so much.'

Total silence followed these words and Niccolò knew he should say something in response, but... He shook his head, for the change taking place in his heart and his head was so seismic that for a moment he couldn't think. All he could do was feel. He stared at her. At the softness of her lips and her eyes as the truth of their situation came slamming home—and what a truth it was. She didn't want his money, but she wanted his baby. And she wanted him. Him. The man beneath all the trappings.

She was the purest, sweetest thing which had happened to him in a lifetime spent trying to bury his pain by papering it over with money and 'success'. But Lizzie had seen beyond that. She'd looked inside him and seen him, and she loved him. His heart stabbed with pain and joy and recognition, because wasn't it time to tell her his final secret? To reveal the mind-blowing impact she'd had on him from the get-go?

'You know something?' he said huskily. 'The day we met was the anniversary of my mother and my sister's deaths.' He paused to allow the brief sting of tears to pass. 'A day I always reserved for something to distract me and keep me busy. A day of guilt and pain, which inevitably ended with a whisky bottle and the beckon of oblivion. But not this year. You opened the door and looked at me with those big green eyes, and I...' How could he explain what had happened—a famously uptight, high-profile man having sex with a total stranger in a broom cupboard? Didn't the country of his birth have an expression for the love at first sight he had experienced in that moment?

'*Un colpo di fulmine*. I was hit by the thunderbolt,' he explained simply. 'And I've never really recovered from that.' He cleared his throat, and suddenly the words were coming thick and fast. 'But that's good, because I don't want to. I just want to spend the rest of my life with you, Lizzie Bailey. I would prefer to marry you and make you my wife, but if you refuse—then I will accept it. But be certain of one thing. That I will spend the rest of my life trying to change your mind.' He stared at her for a long moment, revelling in the sensation of anticipation and desire heating his blood. 'Now come here,' he said.

'No. You come here.'

'Is this a battle of wills?' he challenged softly.

She gave a lazy and speculative smile, as all her new-found sexual confidence reasserted itself. 'Maybe.'

He crossed the floor to take her in his arms, touching her face and hair and then the curve of his unborn child with trembling fingers, as if he couldn't quite believe she—or the baby—were real. His lips brushed against hers and suddenly he could taste the salt of tears and he couldn't work out if they were hers or his, and only when the kiss had ended did he wipe them away. 'I love you,' he said unsteadily, his fingers tangling with the pliant silk of her fiery hair. 'Even though you drew the most unflattering portrait of me.'

'I knew you didn't like it.'

'Actually, it was very useful. It made me think—do I really look as forbidding as that?'

She tilted her head to one side. 'Only some of the time. But not at this precise moment, that's for sure.'

He gave up on conversation then and pulled her closer still, his heart kicking in his chest as his baby kicked beneath her breast.

EPILOGUE

'IS HE ASLEEP?'

Niccolò's gaze travelled across the room to the window seat to where his wife sat, bathed in a pool of gold from the nearby lamp. Her green dress matched her eyes and the giant Christmas tree framed in the window as she finished tying a scarlet ribbon around a present. Behind her, thick snow was falling and the newly white grounds of the Jacobean mansion appeared silvery bright in the moonlight. If it looked like a perfect scene, that was because it was, he thought with a sense of satisfaction. Upstairs lay their beloved son, now almost five years old, clutching a toy puppy called Pesto.

Lizzie looked up and smiled, her hair falling over her shoulder. 'Is he asleep?'

'Like a cherub,' he affirmed as he walked across the room towards her. 'I told him Babbo Natale would not come to visit children unless they were fast asleep.'

'That's what I said earlier, but he wouldn't listen to me. He's such a Daddy's boy.' She gave a contented sigh. 'And did you tell him that tomorrow we can build a snowman?'

'Yes, my love, we can build a snowman,' he answered indulgently, sinking down onto the window seat beside her, because didn't all parents live out their longings through their children? He put his hand on her knee. 'So, what would you like to do now?'

'Oh, I don't know,' she murmured as she pushed the present aside. 'I'm open to all suggestions.'

'Well…' Slowly, he stroked his finger over one silk-covered thigh. 'We could go and drink a glass of champagne before dinner.'

'We could. But there's something much more important we need to do first.'

He knew exactly what she meant, even before she clambered on top of him and wrapped her arms around his neck. She bent her head and kissed him—long and slow and deep—and when the kiss was over, she gazed at him, those incredible green eyes dark with longing and as dazed as they always were whenever they got this close and personal.

'Will it always be this good?' he asked her, his voice suddenly urgent.

'Always,' she affirmed, just as fiercely.

Lizzie hugged him tightly as she felt the powerful beat of his heart against hers, basking in the beauty of her life, because wasn't that what Christmas was all about? About counting your blessings...

It was hard to believe how far they had journeyed and how good it was. The logistics of their new life had taken quite a bit of planning and Niccolò had delegated a stack of stuff to his second-in-command, to concentrate on setting up a new branch of his business in England. It was why they had put extending their little family on hold for the time being, while they got used to their baby and, of course, each other. But they crossed 'the pond' whenever they could, and whenever they were in the States, they stayed in their new house in Westchester, close to Donna and Matt, after Lizzie insisted on moving from the sterile hotel suite, which had never really felt like home.

But it was here—their beautiful house in the Cotswolds—which had claimed both their hearts. They had renovated Ermecott together, moving into the restored manor house shortly after the birth of Federico—a lusty nine-pounder who was the spit of his handsome father. And, yes, there had been a tiny part of her which had worried that Niccolò would find it difficult to get used to fatherhood—a fear dispelled the moment the cord had been severed and her husband had cradled his newborn against his chest, his eyes bright with tears. Lizzie had met his gaze, and she had cried, too.

Her animal portraits had continued to sell to

friends, and friends of friends, but it had been Lizzie's impromptu painting of an adorable mutt from the nearby dogs' home which had changed the trajectory of her life. The picture had been used in a national campaign to make people aware of the pitfalls of buying a pet without thinking it through and the animal's liquid brown eyes, wonky whiskers and slightly anxious-looking mouth had touched a chord with the public. After repeated requests, Lizzie had turned him into a cartoon and these days one of the country's biggest-selling newspapers ran a weekly strip about Pesto, the mongrel. She'd even agreed to help market a slew of dog-related products, the proceeds of which all went to charity. Apart from anything else, it was refreshing to find a pet with an original name!

Somehow, she had found the career she'd always wanted and was so grateful for that, but her priorities were always her son, and her husband—the two true lights of her life. She and Niccolò had married in Manhattan when Federico had been six months old, and honeymooned in Italy, because she'd never been there and had longed to see the land of his birth. They had been staying in the Cinque Terre when she had persuaded him to go and visit his father, who Lizzie had discovered was still alive.

'Why should I?' Niccolò had demanded, his face darkening. 'He won't have anything to say to me, and I certainly won't have anything to say to him.'

But Lizzie had been resolute as she'd watched that old pain clawing at the features of the man she loved. 'It's the courageous thing to do, to confront your demons,' she had insisted quietly. 'To give you the chance to lay them to rest.'

It wasn't what either of them had been expecting. Niccolò's father had lain dying, a broken shell of a man, his cloudy eyes full of tears as he'd touched the face of the young grandson he would never see again. He had spoken in Italian, his words tremulous and faint—but Lizzie hadn't needed to be a linguist to realise how much he'd regretted the past and the way he had behaved towards his son.

Her thoughts cleared as she looked into the jet gleam of Niccolò's eyes.

'Thank you,' he said simply.

'For what?'

'For being the most wonderful mother and wife. For showing me love and how to love. For…' He shook his head, for once seeming uncharacteristically lost for words. 'I love you, Lizzie Macario,' he growled. 'I love you more than words could ever say.'

'And I love you, too. More than you will ever know.' Her throat was thick with emotion as she touched her fingers to the shadowed rasp of his jaw. 'So, we could drink that champagne now, or...'

'Or?' he echoed softly.

'We could start trying for another baby.' She savoured the moment as she met his narrowed gaze.

'You think?' he said huskily.

'Yes. Oh, yes, my darling. I've been thinking it for a while now. And I think you have, too.'

For a long moment he just held her, very tightly, and said something in Italian against her hair, his voice choked with raw emotion. And then he led her from the window seat to the flame-warm rug in front of the fire, a speculative smile curving his lips as, slowly, he began to unbutton her dress.

* * * * *

#4137 NINE MONTHS TO SAVE THEIR MARRIAGE
by Annie West

After his business-deal wife leaves, Jack is intent on getting their on-paper union back on track. He just never imagined their reunion would be *scorching*. Or that their red-hot Caribbean nights would leave Bess *pregnant*! Is this their chance to finally find happiness?

#4138 PREGNANT WITH HER ROYAL BOSS'S BABY
Three Ruthless Kings
by Jackie Ashenden

King Augustine may rule a kingdom, but loyal assistant Freddie runs his calendar. There's no task she can't handle. Except perhaps having to tell her boss she's going to need some time off...because in six months she'll be having *his* heir!

#4139 THE SPANIARD'S LAST-MINUTE WIFE
Innocent Stolen Brides
by Caitlin Crews

Sneaking into ruthless Spaniard Lionel's wedding ceremony, Geraldine arrives just in time to see him being jilted. But Lionel is still in need of a convenient wife...and innocent Geraldine suddenly finds *herself* being led to the altar!

#4140 A VIRGIN FOR THE DESERT KING
The Royal Desert Legacy
by Maisey Yates

After years spent as a political prisoner, Sheikh Riyaz has been released. Now it's Brianna's job to prepare him for his long-arranged royal wedding. But the forbidden attraction flaming between them tempts her to cast duty—and her *innocence*!—to the desert winds...

HPCNMRA0823

#4141 REDEEMED BY MY FORBIDDEN HOUSEKEEPER
by Heidi Rice

Recovering from a near-deadly accident, playboy Renzo retreated to his Côte d'Azur estate. Nothing breaks through his solitude. Until the arrival of his new yet strangely familiar housekeeper, Jessie, stirs dormant desires...

#4142 HIS JET-SET NIGHTS WITH THE INNOCENT
by Pippa Roscoe

When archaeologist Evelyn needs his help saving her professional reputation, Mateo reluctantly agrees. Only the billionaire hadn't bargained on a quest around the world... From Spain to Shanghai, each city holds a different adventure. Yet one thing is constant: their intoxicating attraction!

#4143 HOW THE ITALIAN CLAIMED HER
by Jennifer Hayward

To save his failing fashion house, CEO Cristiano needs the face of the brand, Jensen, to clean up her headline-hitting reputation. But while she's lying low at his Lake Como estate, he's caught between his company...and his desire for the scandalous supermodel!

#4144 AN HEIR FOR THE VENGEFUL BILLIONAIRE
by Rosie Maxwell

Memories of his passion-fueled night with Carrie consume tycoon Damon. Until he discovers the ugly past that connects them and pledges to erase every memory of her. Then she storms into his office...and announces she's carrying his child!

YOU CAN FIND MORE INFORMATION ON UPCOMING HARLEQUIN TITLES, FREE EXCERPTS AND MORE AT HARLEQUIN.COM.

HPCNMRB0823

Get 3 FREE REWARDS!

We'll send you 2 FREE Books plus a FREE Mystery Gift.

FREE
Value Over
$20

Both the **Harlequin® Desire** and **Harlequin Presents®** series feature compelling novels filled with passion, sensuality and intriguing scandals.

HARLEQUIN
PLUS

Try the best multimedia subscription service for romance readers like you!

Read, Watch and Play.

Experience the easiest way to get the romance content you crave.

Start your **FREE TRIAL** at
www.harlequinplus.com/freetrial.